The Brubaker family is back.
This time it's Big Daddy's three hunky nephews
who are in need of some good women.
And nothing is going to stop this proud patriarch
from finding the right little ladies
for his bronco bustin' boys.

THE BRUBAKER BRIDES

THE MILLIONAIRE'S WAITRESS WIFE
(SR#1482 November 2000)

"Some little filly's got me posing as her
working-class groom. She's gonna split a gut
when she discovers her 'husband' is filthy rich."
—Dakota Brubaker

MONTANA'S FEISTY COWGIRL
(SR#1488 December 2000)

"This persistent petunia is posing as a boy—
and she thinks I don't know the truth.
Yee hah, this is gonna be fun!"
—Montana Brubaker

TEX'S EXASPERATING HEIRESS
(SR#1494 January 2001)

"She's the one carting around a million-dollar pig
and she says *I'm* difficult to get along with?"
—Tex Brubaker

Dear Reader,

There's something for *everyone* in a Silhouette Romance, be it moms (or daughters!) or women who've found—or who still seek!—that special man in their lives. Just revel in this month's diverse offerings as we continue to celebrate Silhouette's 20th Anniversary.

It's last stop: STORKVILLE, USA, as Karen Rose Smith winds this adorable series to its dramatic conclusion. A virgin with amnesia finds shelter in the town sheriff's home, but will she find lasting love with *Her Honor-Bound Lawman*? *New York Times* bestselling author Kasey Michaels brings her delightful trilogy THE CHANDLERS REQUEST… to an end with the sparkling bachelor-auction story *Raffling Ryan*. *The Millionaire's Waitress Wife* becomes the latest of THE BRUBAKER BRIDES as Carolyn Zane's much-loved miniseries continues.

In the second installment of Donna Clayton's SINGLE DOCTOR DADS, *The Doctor's Medicine Woman* holds the key to his adoption of twin Native American boys—and to his guarded heart. *The Third Kiss* is a charmer from Leanna Wilson—a must-read pretend engagement story! And a one-night marriage that began with "The Wedding March" leads to *The Wedding Lullaby* in Melissa McClone's latest offering.…

Next month, return to Romance for more of THE BRUBAKER BRIDES and SINGLE DOCTOR DADS, as well as the newest title in Sandra Steffen's BACHELOR GULCH series!

Happy Reading!

Mary-Theresa Hussey

Mary-Theresa Hussey
Senior Editor

Please address questions and book requests to:
Silhouette Reader Service
U.S.: 3010 Walden Ave., P.O. Box 1325, Buffalo, NY 14269
Canadian: P.O. Box 609, Fort Erie, Ont. L2A 5X3

The Millionaire's Waitress Wife

CAROLYN ZANE

SILHOUETTE *Romance*®

Published by Silhouette Books

America's Publisher of Contemporary Romance

For my sisters in the Loveknot, especially Angie, Robin,
Lisa and Karen, for their endless patience and gentle
touch in teaching me so much about the craft of writing.
I love you all.

THANK YOU Dear Lord, for the simple pleasures.

 SILHOUETTE BOOKS

ISBN 0-373-19482-X

THE MILLIONAIRE'S WAITRESS WIFE

Copyright © 2000 by Carolyn Suzanne Pizzuti

Books by Carolyn Zane

CAROLYN ZANE

lives with her husband, Matt, their preschool-age daughter, Madeline and their latest addition, baby daughter, Olivia, in the rolling countryside near Portland Oregon's Willamette River. Like Chevy Chase's character in the movie *Funny Farm*, Carolyn finally decided to trade in a decade of city dwelling and producing local television commercials for the quaint country life of a novelist. And, even though they have bitten off decidedly more than they can chew in the remodeling of their hundred-plus-year-old farmhouse, life is somewhat saner for her than for poor Chevy. The neighbors are friendly, the mail carrier actually stops at the box and the dog, Bob Barker, sticks close to home.

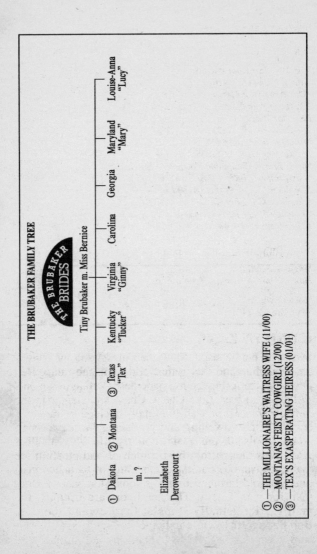

THE BRUBAKER FAMILY TREE

THE BRUBAKER BRIDES

Tiny Brubaker m. Miss Bernice

① Dakota   ② Montana   ③ Texas "Tex"   Kentucky "Tucker"   Virginia "Ginny"   Carolina   Georgia   Maryland "Mary"   Louise-Anna "Lucy"

m. ?

Elizabeth Derovencourt

① — THE MILLIONAIRE'S WAITRESS WIFE (11/00)
② — MONTANA'S FEISTY COWGIRL (12/00)
③ — TEX'S EXASPERATING HEIRESS (01/01)

Chapter One

The cowbell jangled as Dakota Brubaker pushed through the glass doors of the crowded hole-in-the-wall that was Ned's Lonestar Grill. His lanky stride purposeful, his probing gaze searching, he didn't notice the welcoming blast of cool air that greeted him on this blistering hot Texas day. Nor did he notice the greasy aroma of Ned's special half-pound Longhorn Burgers, or the staticky strains of the country-and-western song that played on the radio. He did not see the faded rodeo wallpaper, the tacky art, or the campy plastic plants that hung from the ceiling by macramé holders.

And, most amazingly, as he moved to the counter and settled his lean-from-bustin'-broncs-and-punchin'-cows frame onto the red Naugahyde and chrome stool, Dakota Brubaker did not notice the appreciative glances of the entire female patronage at Ned's.

No, Dakota—infamous flirt and, at age thirty, Hidden Valley's most eligible bachelor—did not notice any of

these things because his senses were already being filled.
Filled by Elizabeth Derovencourt, Ned's newest waitress.

Elizabeth Derovencourt.

Even her lyrical name screamed class. Grace. Style.

Mesmerized, Dakota plucked a tattered menu from between the sugar jar and the napkin dispenser and pretended
to study the selection he already knew by heart. Peripheral
vision afforded him furtive peeks toward the object of his
interest.

At the moment, she was standing behind the counter, a
pencil jammed into her thick, honey-blond bun. Stray ten-
drils of hair had worked their way loose from the clip and
framed her delicate face. A light flush warmed her cheeks
and spoke of her tireless work ethic. Her apron was spattered and somewhat worse for the wear, but to Dakota, she
was stunning.

For a nanosecond, his gaze connected with hers as she
made a fresh pot of coffee and a flash fire ignited and
sizzled down his spine.

She smiled and nodded, acknowledging his presence.

Dakota's knuckles whitened as he gripped his menu. He
returned her nod and favored her with his signature grin;
a slight curl to the upper lip that he knew had the deep
Brubaker dimples bracketing the corners of his mouth. The
signature grin, coupled with a nonchalant—at least he
hoped it was nonchalant, it was hard to tell his heart was
making such a ruckus in his chest—lift of his brow, usually
had the women swooning.

Elizabeth turned her attention back to the coffeemaker.

Okay. Dakota rotated his shoulders to release some tension. So the signature grin and nonchalant brow lift didn't
exactly have her falling at his feet.

She was a challenge. She didn't seem interested in him.
Or anyone else, for that matter.

He liked that about her.

Dakota didn't know much about Elizabeth yet. But he intended to learn as much as possible, as fast as possible. Already, he'd asked around and the regulars at Ned's had filled him in on a few key details. She'd only lived in Hidden Valley for two months, she was originally from Dallas, she wasn't much on talking about her family, she was twenty-seven years old and, most important of all, she was single and unattached.

Amazing.

"I'll be right with you." Her husky, sexy voice reached him as she swished past, arms loaded with plates of burgers and fries.

Dakota gave his head a confident nod and, with another signature grin, forced himself not to stare. "Take your time," he tossed over his shoulder, but didn't mean a word of it.

She didn't respond.

That was okay. She was busy. Dakota took the opportunity to further his studies.

After much keen observation during the many lunch hours he'd spent at the Lonestar since Elizabeth had been hired, he was putting a few pieces of the curvaceous puzzle together in his mind. From firsthand experience, he knew that she always smelled of talcum powder, spearmint gum and some kind of fruity shampoo.

He'd also learned that she favored pop music over county and western because of the way she changed the radio station every time Ned took a cigarette break. Sometimes, the rhythm would grab hold of her body, she would dance, hips swaying, across the worn linoleum, between the pickup window and the booths. Her off-key humming would bring good-natured smiles to her customers' faces. She was fun to talk to, and when the lunch crowd thinned, she would loiter at the counter and keep him company while she filled salt shakers and catsup bottles.

He'd discovered that she could tell wonderful jokes, that she was sassy and sensitive and that she was as beautiful on the inside as she was on the out.

And, he was reasonably sure—as sketchy and one-dimensional as this portrait was—that she was the one.

The one.

The one who could convince him to give up the good life, for married life.

Not now, of course. But some time, in the distant future.

"Hi, Dakota. Sorry about the wait." Frazzled, Elizabeth moved up to the counter, slipped the pencil from her bun and looked at him with expectation. "What'll it be today?"

Emerging from his reverie where Elizabeth starred as the future Mrs. Dakota Brubaker, he bestowed her once again with his signature grin, and this time, she responded in kind.

"The usual."

"Longhorn burger, medium-well, extra pickles, no onions, side of fries, coffee, black."

"Yep." He nodded. *And, a date sometime this weekend,* he wanted to add, but decided to bide his time until the place thinned out and he had her attention all to himself. "Busy today?"

Elizabeth exhaled long and slow and cocked her hip against the counter. "Mmm." She glanced at the clock on the wall. "But it's almost over. Thank heavens. I could really use a break. My dogs are barkin'." She pointed at her feet with the eraser tip of her pencil.

Dakota patted the empty red Naugahyde stool at his side. "Why don't you sit down and rest for a few minutes?"

The gentle hubbub of the dining room was indeed winding down. Her gaze traveled from booth to booth and Dakota watched as she scanned the needs of the customers, then nodded. "I could do that. For a minute. I missed my morning break, so I don't think Ned will mind."

Dakota was glad. This might be a good opportunity to ask her out. He hoped she was free tonight. There was a good movie playing down at the Bijou.

Her deep gaze, the color of midnight sky, focused on him as she settled herself on the stool. She cupped her jaw in the palm of her hand and rested her elbow on the countertop. "So, what's new?"

"Oh, I don't know. A lot of typical ranch stuff." He shrugged, wondering how interesting she'd find his routine.

"So, tell me. What's a typical day like for you?" Since she seemed genuinely curious, he sat up a little straighter.

"Well, I have to go to a cattle auction this afternoon. Tomorrow, I have to shuffle a bunch of papers and clean out my office. It's a pit."

"But tomorrow is Saturday."

"Ranch don't stop runnin' on the weekends. Next week is really gonna be busy. We have to brand some cattle, break some horses, mend some fences out in the south section and...hmm, oh yeah," just remembering, he made a mental note, "I've gotta have the vet come out. Time for blackfly shots."

"You work for the...er, the Circle K, right?"

He chuckled. "Close. No, I work for the Circle BO. It's about fifteen minutes outside of town. I'm the foreman out there."

"The foreman, ahhh." An admiration filled her eyes that had his pulse kicking up a notch. "That sounds like fun."

He lifted his shoulder in an aw-shucks manner. "It's okay. We all get a chance to run the ranch at one time or another."

"Who is we-all?"

"My cousins and brothers. Maybe you've heard of my uncle? Big Daddy Brubaker?" Everyone around these parts knew Big Daddy.

A slight frown marred her brow. "Can't say that I have, but that's not unusual, me being new to these parts and all. I don't know very many people in Hidden Valley yet."

Dakota bit back a smile. How refreshing. She still didn't know diddly about the infamous and exceedingly wealthy Brubaker family. It was so nice to simply talk to a beautiful woman and not wonder if she had dollar signs swimming before her eyes. Dakota had been burned by more than one fortune hunter in his time. Elizabeth was such a welcome change of pace.

She tucked a few loose strands of hair back up into her bun. "You worked there long?"

"'Bout a year. Ever since my cousin Johnny got married."

A faraway, dreamy look crossed her face. "Running a ranch sounds like fun. As a kid, I always wanted to live on a ranch. I adored horses. In fact…I had every…horse book that…"

Distracted by the cowbell signaling the arrival of another patron, her gaze shifted to the door and her voice trailed off. As Dakota waited for her to continue, he entertained visions of her as a young, horse-loving girl. Much the way he envisioned their daughter would look someday.

Her exasperated sigh popped his little fantasy bubble and he followed her doleful gaze with his own to a man standing just inside the door.

The stranger appeared to be about his age, Dakota figured, probably somewhere in his late twenties, early thirties. He looked crisp and cool despite the stifling weather, resplendent—albeit out of place—in his designer togs. A black, leather bag hung by a strap over his shoulder, resting at his hip and an expensive pair of sunglasses dangled from between his teeth. Though it was obvious that he was trying to fit in with the casual atmosphere of the diner, he was clearly ill at ease and considered himself to be slumming. His haughty gaze roved the room until it landed upon Elizabeth. A strained smile touched his lips and he moved to the counter.

The T-shirt and denim wearing crowd at Ned's Lonestar Grill stared at him as if he'd just disembarked from a spaceship out front.

Elizabeth fairly vibrated with awareness.

Competition? Dakota didn't know, but he could hardly believe that his saintly Elizabeth would go for such a pompous doofus.

"Elizabeth."

"Charles."

"I've been looking for you." Charles's voice was deep and cultured. He glanced at the empty stool at her other side with disdain, before he perched on its edge. "In fact, I've been looking since the day you left, nearly two months ago."

"I've no doubt."

"Figured I'd eventually catch up with you." Charles studied his manicure.

Elizabeth sighed. "And so you have."

"I've come to take you home."

Morbid fascination held Dakota in his seat. So. His future wife had a boyfriend. Or worse, a husband. Fiery needles knitted his guts into knots. So much for asking her out on a date. A feeling of restlessness dictated that he adjust his position. He stood and, spinning the stool between his legs, straddled it backwards. Chin propped on the backrest, Dakota settled in to listen. Might as well find out what he could about the fish that got away.

"We've been over this before, Charles. I'm not going home."

Charles shot an annoyed glance over Elizabeth's shoulder to Dakota. "Do you mind?"

"No. I don't mind. Go right ahead."

Though Dakota knew this conversation didn't concern him, he was unable to mind his own business. There was something suddenly vulnerable about Elizabeth. Something that brought out his protective streak. He dug around in his shirt pocket, and made a show out of opening a new pack of gum. Spearmint. The brand she favored. He offered a piece to Charles.

Charles ignored him.

Elizabeth took a stick and smiled in gratitude. Dakota grinned. Smarmy husband or no, Elizabeth would have his devotion forever.

"Victoria is sick. Maybe dying." Charles waited for Elizabeth to digest his dramatic announcement as she thoughtfully chewed her gum.

Elizabeth rolled her eyes in a world-weary fashion. "Charles, Victoria is always sick and dying. You're going to have to come up with something better than that old ploy to lure me back into the pit of vipers."

"I'm serious, Elizabeth. She's very ill."

"As it suits her purpose."

"Elizabeth, it's time to stop this ridiculous game you are playing."

"What game?"

"Your running away from the family fortune."

"It's not a game."

Brow lifted, Dakota's gaze roved over Elizabeth, appraising the exasperated look in her eye and the spattered apron. *Family fortune?*

"You can't be serious." Charles's voice took on a

whiny quality that Dakota felt lessened the aristocratic presentation.

He stopped chewing his gum and watched in fascination as Charles's pointy Adam's apple bobbed up and down. The old boy was beginning to lose a bit of his cool facade. Jaw grim, Charles strained toward Elizabeth. Dakota followed suit.

"Elizabeth, you are coming back with me today." His words were clipped, nearly threatening. "As her only granddaughter, you have no choice. Victoria wants you to inherit now. She's ready to retire and to turn the company over to you. If you don't cooperate, she'll no doubt give her fortune to…to…who knows who! Then where will we all be? You have to come to grips with reality. It's time for you to marry Bernard and settle down."

Bernard? Dakota's gaze snapped from Charles to Elizabeth. *Who the heck was Bernard?*

Elizabeth hooted in a most unsociety-like fashion. "Charles, you know that Victoria would never give her precious company away. She is simply using it as a tool to manipulate me, and it won't work. And, if you're laboring under the delusion that I'll someday marry that wimpy Bernard, you can stop."

"Why not?"

"Well, for one thing, I don't love him."

"You know Victoria will never accept such a lame reason."

"Oh, yeah?"

Charles lifted an elegant brow.

Bristling like a porcupine, Elizabeth stared at Charles. "Oh…yeah?" Her mouth worked and her eyes blazed as she clearly groped for a more scathing rebuke. "Well, I have other reasons for not marrying Bernard. Very, very good reasons."

"And those are?"

"Okay…" She cleared her throat.

"Yes?"

Dakota resisted the urge to cheer her on, but he did reach out to give her arm a reassuring pat. She clutched his hand and gave it a grateful squeeze. Then, a slow smile crossed her face as something seemed to click in her brain.

"Okay, I didn't want to have to break it to you this way, but… It really doesn't matter if Victoria won't accept that I don't love Bernard, because—" Elizabeth leaned forward and poked Charles in the chest "—I'm already married!"

Charles blanched. "You are not."

"Am too."

Gaze skeptical, Charles leaned back. "To whom?"

"To…to…I'm married to…" she spun in her stool to face Dakota, her expression beseeching him not to betray her, "I'm married to him." She looped an arm around Dakota's neck and pressing her cheek to his, turned to face her brother.

"Charles, I'd like you to meet your brother-in-law, Dakota Brubaker. Dakota, darling, this is my older brother, Charles Derovencourt."

Dakota nearly swallowed his gum.

Chapter Two

Elizabeth held her breath and waited for what seemed like an eternity for Dakota to respond. She knew she'd really put the poor guy on the spot. But, though she didn't know him well, she knew he was single and fun loving and…there. Knuckles white, she clutched his collar and, pressing her face to his, willed him not to betray her. She could feel his breathing quicken as she slid off her stool to stand next to him.

A slow smile crept across Dakota's mouth. "Well now. This *is* a surprise." He glanced at her, then back at her brother. "I'm…pleased to meet you, Chuck." He held out his hand, then let it drop when Charles did not reciprocate.

A shadow of uncertainty darkened Charles's aristocratic features. "You are *not* married to him."

"Yes, I am." She closed her eyes and urged Dakota to read her mind. As far as she was concerned, he only need go along with this little charade long enough to get rid of Charles. Once Charles was convinced that she was serious about not returning, he would carry the shocking news of her marriage to Victoria. And then, knowing her family's prejudice against unions outside their elite social circle, she would be disowned. *Hallelujah!* Free at last. "Tell him, honey," Elizabeth urged, and hoped that Dakota's good sense of humor wouldn't fail him now.

It didn't.

She could feel his dimples bloom against her cheek and the slight rasp of his stubbled jaw was curiously pleasant.

"Married? Oh, sure. Been married for a long time. Let's see…" Still straddling the stool, Dakota tugged Elizabeth down upon his knee and snaked an arm around her waist. Brow drawn, he reared back slightly, to better see her. "I'm bad with anniversaries. How long has it been, now, sugar lips?"

"Uh, well, now, um…okay…" She hadn't expected him to toss the curve ball back to her court quite so soon, but she wasn't going to quibble. Beggars couldn't be choosers. He was trying to help and for that, she would be forever grateful. Realizing that she was mangling the placket of Dakota's western shirt, she relaxed her grip and smoothed the soft, well-bleached denim with her fingertips. "Uh, hasn't it been nearly a month?"

"You've been married for a month?" Eyes narrowed with skepticism, Charles glanced back and forth between the two of them.

"Has it been that long already?" Dakota pretended to muse. "We got married back in June…."

"July. It's August." Elizabeth gave his nose what she hoped appeared to be a wifely tweak and his twinkling eyes had the blood rushing to her cheeks. She touched her tongue to her lips. Sitting so close to him this way was unnerving. He exuded the kind of raw, male sensuality that was difficult to ignore. And, though he had the steely build of a genuine cowboy, the arms that circled her waist were gentle.

"Right. What was I thinking? We got married in July."

"July the thirty—"

"Second…"

The thirty-second? Where was he going with this? She nudged him in the arm with her elbow. If they were going to get rid of Charles, they needed to stay credible. She pasted a smile on her face. "How could you forget, darling? It was July *twenty*-second."

"That's just what I said."

"It is not."

"Yes it is."

"No, you said—"

"Honey," he arched a suggestive brow and pouted, "you know I hate it when we fight."

Elizabeth blushed and resisted the urge to laugh at his comical expression. "Me, too."

"It was a beautiful wedding, Chuck, too bad you couldn't attend—" Dakota seemed to squint off into the blissful past.

"But, of course you couldn't because we didn't invite *anyone*. Because, well, because we eloped, so it was just the two of us."

Dakota began to really get into his role. "And Elvis."

"Elvis?" She nudged him a little harder this time.

"That little chapel in Vegas? With that Elvis impersonator? The one who hitched your star to mine?"

"Right, right. Just you, me and…" she cleared her throat and warned him with her eyes not to get too carried away, "Elvis."

"And our love."

"Of course." She turned in Dakota's embrace and beamed at her brother. "Our love."

Charles snorted in derision. "Love? Oh, please."

She frowned. "Dakota, darling, I don't think Charles believes us."

"Are you trying to say that our marriage is a farce?" Dakota affected a similarly wounded expression. "Well, now, that hurts, doesn't it, hon?"

"Yes. It does."

Though he'd never admit it, Elizabeth could tell that the seeds of doubt were beginning to take root in the back of Charles's mind. If she'd run away from a fortune to work in a greasy spoon simply to rebel, would eloping with a cowboy be so far-fetched? She didn't think he would think so.

In fact, this was brilliant.

Why hadn't she thought of it before? An ill-suited match to a laid-back and salt-of-the-earth guy like Dakota, would probably get her disinherited faster than all the other she-nanigans she'd pulled over the years put together. She could see Charles noting the faded jeans, the worn cowboy boots, the muscular build and deep tan that came from hard work under a hot sun. He was judging Dakota as surely as Victoria would. They would both dismiss him without ever really getting to know him.

And why?

Because he was working class.

Her brother regarded them through suspicious eyes. "You can't have known each other for more than a couple months. If you are married, and I am not convinced that you are, the attraction is not love."

"Chuck, sounds to me like now you're trying to insinuate that I married her for her money."

A muscle twitched in Charles's eye.

"Let me put your fears to rest, Chuck. I may not own a fancy purse, like the one you're sporting there—"

Feathers ruffled, Charles drew his chin into his neck. "It's a communication system."

"—whatever—but I'm reasonably well fixed. My truck is paid off, and I have a good job on my uncle's little spread. Before I tied the knot with your sister, I had my own bunk and everything."

Elizabeth tried to arrange her expression into one of serene marital bliss, as Dakota explained their relationship to her brother.

"It's obvious that you've never really been in love before, Chuck old boy, or you'd be able to see that what your sister and I have goin' isn't something you can hang a price tag on. Right, darlin'?"

He emitted an amorous growl from deep within his throat that had Elizabeth going suddenly limp in his arms.

"Oh, I'll admit that in the beginning, I found her irresistible on a very physical level. Wanted to kiss her from the moment I laid eyes on her. But—" he reached up and cupping her jaw in his work-roughened hand, turned her face to his "—after I got to know her, it wasn't long before I knew she was the one I wanted to spend the rest of my life with."

The air whooshed from Elizabeth's lungs. Wow. This guy was good. If she didn't know better, she'd be tempted to think he was serious. The way he was looking at her with those intense, thundercloud gray eyes that had her heart pounding beneath her breast. A curious buzzing echoed in her suddenly light head, and her entire body felt as if she'd been leaning against an electric fence.

Her gaze clung to Dakota's as her brother looked on in disgust.

"All right, fine, Elizabeth. You've had your fun. You can have this mistake annulled. Bernard will forgive you. He still wants to marry you."

"Hey now—" Dakota frowned.

"Charles. Haven't you been listening? I can't."

"And I can't be responsible for what this will do to Victoria."

"She's a lot tougher than you give her credit for, Charles."

"Not anymore. Not since you left. She's been very depressed. Weak."

Elizabeth ground her teeth. For pity's sake, why did this always happen to her? Just when she thought she'd found a way to lead her own life, her family would snatch her back into their clutches. Charles still knew how to push all the right buttons to make her feel guilty.

"Elizabeth, at the very least, you owe Victoria an explanation. In person. Run and get your things together and come back to Dallas with me and make amends. Before it's…" he let the ominous tone of his words sink in, "…too late."

With that last edict, Charles stood and flicked some imaginary bits of lint off the creases in his perfectly pressed, khaki pants.

She glanced helplessly to Dakota then back to Charles. She could feel herself being manipulated yet again by her powerful family, and she resented it. Yet how could she say no? What if Charles was telling the truth and Victoria was really dying? Despite the fact that her cranky old grandmother wanted to run her life, Elizabeth loved her, and would regret not taking the opportunity to say goodbye.

Then again, what if this was just another plot to haul her back to the prison they all called home? It wouldn't be the first time.

"Charles, I can't just up and leave with you tonight," she hedged, buying time, wracking her brain for a way to return on her own terms. She would not be hauled back like a recalcitrant child.

"Why not?"

"Because I have obligations, that's why! To my job. To my," she patted Dakota's granite bicep, "my..."

"Your better half," Dakota supplied. The tiny lines at the corners of his eyes forked. "Your knight in shining armor? Your..." he buried his nose in her hair, his breath hot, his voice husky. It was clear he was enjoying himself far more than was absolutely necessary, *"...lover."*

"Uh...yes. Thank you, dear." She pinched his thumb just hard enough to let him know that if he didn't stop she was going to start laughing hysterically and ruin everything.

"This is a family emergency, Elizabeth. Under the circumstances, I'm sure your boss will understand."

Dakota tightened his grip around her waist. "She's not going anywhere without me."

"How touching." Charles prepared to leave. "Shall I tell Grandmother to expect you both?"

Elizabeth's heart stopped. Charles had thrown down the gauntlet.

And, Dakota recklessly picked it up.

"Why, thank you, for the heartfelt invite, Chuck. I'll be there. With spurs on." Dakota rested his chin on her shoulder and shot her an expectant look.

Jaw slack, Elizabeth reared back and stared at Dakota. Was he kidding? Bluffing? Crazy? She tried to swallow. Okay, maybe they'd gone just a bit too far. Telling Charles she was married to Dakota was one thing. Bringing him home to meet Victoria was jumping out of the frying pan and into the bowels of Hades. "Now, honey, we have to go to that cow auction, remember?" Her smile was thousand-watt. "That's *important* to your *career,* and we *don't* want to miss it."

"But I'd skip the auction for you, babe."

Brows raised, eyes wide, she forced the words through her teeth, hoping to communicate her extreme opposition. "Won't you get into *trouble?* You *don't* want to get *fired.*"

"I'm the boss remember? I can go to an auction any old time."

"But, *honey* what about all of those…ranch things you have to do? *You know,* the vet is flying out with the *black shots* and what about all of those *broken horses?*"

Dakota frowned, bewildered.

Charles grew weary of their debate. "Fine. I'll expect you both to travel with me." He rummaged in his communications bag for his phone.

"Whoa. If Elizabeth decides to go, I'll drive her," Dakota said. "I have my truck."

"As you wish." Charles shrugged.

"Okay, you guys, now hold on just a minute. I, uh, I'll have to ask Ned about a sub for tomorrow…"

Before Charles could respond, Ned craned his head out the order window and shouted, "Elizabeth, your deluxe burger baskets are up." At the same time, a group of customers formed a line at the cash register and tapped the bell for service.

Ned's gravelly voice had jolted her back to reality and she eased out of Dakota's lap and moved to do her job. "I have to get back to work."

With a glance at his watch Charles gathered his bag and sunglasses. "I'll tell Victoria that you will be home by eight. We'll expect you for dinner."

Elizabeth sighed and nodded. "All right." She would

figure this out later, when she was away from the intoxicating Dakota.

Half an hour later, Dakota watched as Elizabeth rang up the last of the lunch rush. The Lonestar was now empty, with the exception of a few stragglers who nursed their coffee and read the paper in booths near the back. Slowly revolving ceiling fans circulated the aroma of freshly brewed coffee.

Dakota sighed and pushed back his plate.

What on earth had he been thinking, offering to go with her to Dallas this weekend? Pulling one over on stuffy old Chuck here at Ned's had been one thing, but the idea of going with her as her husband to meet the family was...well, insane. She'd tried to talk him out of it, even came up with some handy excuses to get him off the hook. But oh, no. He'd put his mouth in gear before his brain and practically insisted on going.

It was just that something about Elizabeth brought out an extreme chivalrous streak in him. He'd been able to sense the urgency in her from the moment her brother had entered the diner, and he'd wanted to help. Unfortunately, in his zeal to bail out this damsel in distress, he may have made matters even worse.

It was clear that she had her reasons for not wanting him to go home with her. His mind working, Dakota shifted in his seat. What a chump. She probably wanted to kill him. Now he'd never get that date.

It sure had been great to hold Elizabeth in his arms, though. To spend a few unforgettable minutes being her husband. To get a real feel for the future that he'd dreamed of so often, of late. Mmm-hum.

Back in the kitchen, Ned took off his apron, hung it over a peg and headed out back for a cigarette.

Elizabeth turned the radio station from country and western to pop and joined him at the counter to perform her after-lunch chores.

"Listen, Dakota, about what happened with my brother," she shot an apologetic glance at him as she rinsed a cloth in bleach water and began to wipe down and polish the chrome napkin dispensers. "I'm so sorry that I dragged you into the middle of my little power struggle with my family. It's just that I was desperate to lash out at him, and telling him that I was married to you seemed like a good idea at the time."

"Sure." Though the compliment was backhanded, Dakota beamed. She was just so darned cute.

"I didn't mean to put you on the spot." Little droplets fell from her cloth and scattered across the Formica countertop as she worked. "Anyway, thanks for helping me out. That was really nice of you."

"No problem. I hope I didn't get too carried away by promising him a bunch of stuff that, well, you didn't want to do."

"No, no. You were perfect."

Dakota relaxed a little. Maybe all was not lost after all.

"Think we fooled him?" she asked.

"I don't know. Did you really want to? Or were you just trying to get rid of him?"

"A little of both, I suppose."

He laughed. "So. If you don't mind my asking, what exactly is going on?"

"Oh, I don't mind at all." She sighed and twisted her cleaning cloth around her fingers. "I'm trying to get written out of my grandmother's will."

He cocked a curious brow. "Written out of her will? Why?"

"I know, it sounds crazy. It's a long story. Suffice it to

say that she wants to control me and she thinks her money is the key to keeping me where she wants me. Trouble is—'' she lowered her voice to a whisper and made a face ''—I hate money.''

The fact that she wasn't a gold digger was great news. Although—Dakota adjusted his position to ease the sudden tension he felt assault him between the shoulder blades—maybe now was not the best time to tell her about his own family's vast fortune. He'd tell her later, when Charles's visit wasn't quite so fresh.

''Anyway,'' she continued, ''over the years, I've tried everything I know how to get her to disown me. Recently, I've been trying to scandalize my way out of the family. I thought I'd succeeded by moving here two months ago, renting a little single-wide trailer down on the wrong side of the tracks and taking a job as a waitress in a greasy spoon. But, apparently, that didn't do the trick. I'm,'' she peered up at him and flashed him a sheepish smile, ''hoping that my recent marriage to you will.''

''Why would telling your family you're married to me be a scandal?''

Bright spots of pink flared on her cheeks and her eyes darted about in embarrassment. ''Because you are everything my family would loathe in a husband for me.''

Dakota pinched his lips. She really didn't have a clue who he was.

She touched his arm in a gesture of apology and her words tumbled over each other. ''Don't get me wrong. I think you're great, just the way you are. As a matter of fact, you're living the life I've always wanted to live, out in the country with the horses and the cows and the flies and stuff. Please, don't take offense.''

''None taken.'' Dakota shook his head. This was definitely a first. Usually, when he went home with a girl to meet her family, he felt like a trophy that had been bagged in a high-stakes hunt. The fact that Elizabeth's family would not be standing on their heads to entice him to join their ranks was curiously exhilarating.

Water rained from the cloth as she wrung it out, more from a need to vent excess energy than any real need to clean. "I'm not ready for commitment yet," she declared vehemently. "And when the time comes, I want to choose my own husband. This isn't the Dark Ages. With the exception of my late mother and father, arranged marriages have made all of my relatives miserable. I won't be railroaded into making the same mistake."

This was encouraging. "Gonna let Bernard wriggle off the hook, huh?"

"You got that right." Grin saucy, she dropped her rag in the pail. "I'd rather marry a *Saint* Bernard."

Dakota laughed. "So, what do you plan to do now?"

"Obviously, I haven't thought that far in advance. I'd jump out of the window, but," her grin was rueful, "we are on the ground level."

He laughed. "Going home would be that bad, huh?"

"Well, let's just say that my family puts the 'fun' in dysfunction." With a weary huff, she began stuffing napkins into their now shiny chrome holder. "But, I guess I have to go now. Victoria thinks she can just decide to announce that she's dying, and I'll come running. And, of course, she's right."

Dakota's heart went out to her. He didn't know all of the details, but her family sounded like a real piece of work. The Brubaker clan was wonderful and loving and he was close with not only his own family, but with his uncle Big Daddy's family as well. It was hard to imagine, wanting to run away from family. He could only guess that the situation must be pretty grim, for her to go to such lengths. And, if Charles was any indication, it was.

"I hope I didn't screw everything up for you by telling your brother that I'd come home with you."

"No, no. I'll just…I'll—" she smiled and shrugged, and seemed to suddenly come to terms with something she'd been wrestling with since Charles had departed. "Listen, Dakota, I've been thinking." She picked up the napkin dispenser and held it in front of her chest, as if bracing herself. "I know this is going to sound very forward, and more than a little crazy, but how would you like to earn some extra money this weekend?"

He schooled his face into a mask of mild interest, and wondered what on earth she was up to now. "Could always use a few extra bucks, I guess. What do you have in mind?"

With a deep, fortifying breath, Elizabeth plunged ahead. "I would like to hire you to come with me to my grandmother's house as my husband."

Chapter Three

By four o'clock that afternoon, Dakota was home, in the two bedroom bunkhouse he shared with his younger brother, Montana, out at the Circle BO. Small, but comfortable, the rustic cabin was one of a number of such residences his uncle provided for the hands that worked his ranch. Clustered together under a grove of trees, the grouping resembled a summer camp for cowboys.

Inside the main living area of his bunkhouse, Dakota was rooting through a storage trunk that doubled as a coffee table. A beat up leather duffel bag sat open on the floor next to the couch and as he packed, he silently berated himself.

How had he allowed himself to get talked into this debacle?

A pair of eyes the color of a tropical sea, that's how.

When Elizabeth had first asked him if he would go with her, he'd said yes, without giving it a second thought. It was impossible for him to deny her anything, when she batted those baby blues at him.

Now that he'd had a little time to step back and review the situation in a calm, rational manner, he had to admit the whole idea was nuts. But she'd been persuasive. Very, very persuasive. He replayed their earlier conversation in his mind, rehashing, trying to figure out how he'd ended up in this mess.

"It's just for the weekend," she'd cajoled. "Two, three days tops. I'd be willing to bet that Charles will have already called and warned them that you are coming. If I don't show up with you, they'll wonder."

"We can't have that," he'd heard himself give voice to his impulse.

A girlish, hopeful light flashed in her eyes and he ignored the niggling feeling of warning it triggered. "I have a savings account. I would certainly reimburse you for your time."

That last part had amused him, but he hadn't let on. Instead, like a love-struck fool, he'd smiled and encouraged her to continue.

"Dakota, this isn't the first time that they have done this to me. Whenever Victoria fears that I'm straying a little too far afield, she comes down with an incurable disease. Then I end up promising her the moon and resenting it. I have a feeling that this time, she is no closer to dying than I am. Well, I'm sick of being manipulated like some kind of puppet. I have a right to live my life as I see fit. And, if I want to be poor, that's my business."

He couldn't fault her there. Even in his own family, Big Daddy made sure that all of his children, nieces and nephews included, had a chance to indulge in a little hard labor, before they took their places among the corporate ranks in one of the family companies. A taste of real life made a better executive, his uncle claimed.

And, he knew Big Daddy was right.

"Maybe, if we can make Victoria see how, uh, you know, happy you make me, she will back off."

Maybe.

Dakota exhaled slowly as he surveyed the contents of the trunk that was filled with memories and garb from his rodeo days. The fact that he was expected to join her for the weekend in Dallas was as much his doing as hers. He'd practically demanded that they go together. Growing philosophical in his reverie, he unearthed a set of silver spurs and they clanked as he dropped them to the floor. He'd also let her hoity-toity brother get under his skin. Charles's controlling attitude had certainly helped goad him into this lunacy.

So now he was going home to meet her folks. Something he hadn't planned on doing for a long, long time. At least not until they'd had some more time to get to know each other. To date. To become a couple.

Oh, well. It was too late to back out now. Elizabeth was counting on him.

Since he couldn't seem to marshal his gray matter when she was in the room, he'd agreed to hire on and act according to her wishes. Helpless to deny her anything, he'd given her his vow. To have and to hold, to play the part of the unsuitable suitor for better or worse, until the end of the weekend. Or death parted them. Whichever came first. Dakota ran a hand over his jaw. At this point, he feared the outcome was a toss-up.

With a dubious grin he recalled her packing suggestions. A kooky hodgepodge, considering they were headed for the city. To Elizabeth, the fact that he was a dirt-poor cowpoke was one of his most valuable attributes when it came to scandalizing her grandmother. It seemed that if he showed up at Victoria's looking like someone who would frequent the Longbranch and date Miss Kitty, so much the better. He hoped she was joking when she'd suggested he bring a horse.

A couple of bright bandannas, two gaudy bolo ties, and a silver belt buckle as big as a dinner plate joined the spurs on the floor. An old pair of brightly decorated rodeo chaps lay in the bottom of the trunk and, just for kicks, he dug them out and tried them on for size. After that, he added a holster that he'd hand-tooled in high school art class, a broken revolver that had no bullets and a vest that sported a blue ribbon he'd won for calf roping years ago. Might as well bring this stuff, too.

If the plan was to mess with her grandmother's mind, then he'd surely succeed, in this getup. Head bowed, he looked down at himself and shrugged. What the heck? After all, she'd ordered—and was paying for—a wild man. And he aimed to deliver. He whipped the ancient revolver out of the holster, twirled it on his forefinger and slung it back against his hip in one smooth action. He grinned. Still had the touch. As a kid he'd practiced that move for hours, even though it would never come in handy.

He was punching a Texas bull-ridin' curve into the brim of an old black cowboy hat, when heavy footfalls followed by a loud knock sounded out front. Abandoning his packing project, Dakota popped the hat on his head and moved to the door.

His uncle, Big Daddy Brubaker—diminutive patriarch of the immense Brubaker clan, ranch owner and founder of the Brubaker Oil dynasty—was standing on the cabin's small porch smiling up at him. After his initial greeting, the elfin man's quizzical gaze roved over his nephew's outfit, but he didn't comment.

"You wanted to see me, son?"

"Yessir. Thank you for coming." Dakota invited his uncle inside and motioned for him to take a seat in the living room. After a trip to the refrigerator for a couple of frosty beers, he joined the older man on the couch. Not wanting to go into unnecessary detail, he handed a bottle to his uncle and decided to cut to the chase. "Big Daddy, I need to take the weekend off." Mondays and Tuesdays were his regular days off.

The wiry hairs atop Big Daddy's brow seesawed as he popped the top on his brew. "Any particular reason?"

"I have a—" Dakota cleared his throat "—a date."

"And you need the weekend off?" His uncle's tone was loaded with parental censure.

"It's not like it sounds. Actually, I'm going to Dallas to meet her family and stay with them."

His uncle's pliant face was suddenly wreathed in smiles. Everyone knew that there was nothing on earth that pleased Big Daddy more than knowing his family was in some stage of falling in love. "Well, hot diggity dog, boy! I didn't even know you were seeing anyone special." He held his bottle up in salute and took a congratulatory swig.

"She's very special, sir." Dakota opted not to divulge that this would be their first date.

"She must be, if you're going to meet the family. What's her name?"

"Elizabeth."

"That's nice. Well, I know it's none of my bidness, and you are a fully grown man, but I feel I'd be remiss in my duty as your uncle if I didn't warn you to behave yourself and act like a—" again, his raisin-like gaze surveyed Dakota's odd getup "—Brubaker this weekend."

"You have my word on that."

"Good. When do you plan on leaving?"

"I'm driving her up to Dallas this afternoon as soon as her shift is over, down at Ned's Lonestar Grill. She's a waitress there. Say," elbows on his chaps, Dakota leaned forward and looked at his uncle, "Big Daddy, would you mind if I borrowed that big flatbed rig that we were using to haul hay yesterday, for the weekend?"

"What for?"

"I want to take Elizabeth to Dallas in it."

The older man gaped at him. "You want to drive your girl to Dallas in that old thing, when you have a brand new pickup truck with every luxury? Why?"

"Big Daddy—" Dakota rubbed the calluses on the palm of his hand and wondered how best to explain, "she doesn't go for showy displays of wealth. Her family is...well, her family is—"

"Oh. Say no more. I totally understand."

He did?

Lower lip protruding, eyes narrowed thoughtfully, Big Daddy's head bobbed in a sage manner. "You don't want to pour it on too thick at first."

"Exactly."

"Probably wise. I know our family's good fortune can be intimidating to some folks. But don't worry, son. If she loves you, she and her family won't hold the fact that your daddy and me own a hefty chunk of this state against you."

"Do you really think so?" He wanted to believe that.

"Sure. Seen it happen with my own kids more than once. Just be yourself. I always thought folks who flaunted their wealth were boring anyway. Just stay low-key and give 'em a chance to get to know ya." Big Daddy glanced at his watch. "I gotta go. The missus is expectin' me. You can take the old flatbed if you want. Have a good time, son. And make me and your daddy proud."

"Um-hmm. Thank you, sir. I...will do what I can." A stab of guilt assailed Dakota.

The older man stood to leave, just as Dakota's brother, Montana arrived. As Big Daddy passed Montana on his way to the front door, he paused. "Montana, you'll stand in as foreman for Dakota this weekend."

"I will?"

"Yep."

Montana watched his uncle trot down the front steps to his Land Rover, then closed the door behind him and moved to the couch, where Dakota had resumed packing. He whistled low and long. "Shooee. Aren't you lookin' fly in them fancy chaps?"

"Shut up."

Montana laughed. "Where will you be this weekend? Nerd rodeo?"

"I have a date."

"And you need to pack your spurs?" Amused, Montana lifted a brow and stared at the odd assortment that lay next to the duffel bag. "Must be some date."

"It is." Dakota paused and shook his head. "It's the goofiest date I've ever had."

"And when can we expect you home, young man?"

"Good question." He grabbed a bullwhip, coiled it and thrust it into his bag.

Montana frowned.

Dakota followed his gaze to the whip and laughed. "Oh, that's not for her. It's for her grandmother."

"Yeah, right." Ambling to the couch, Montana guffawed. "Wanna tell me what's going on?"

"Yeah, I'd probably better, so that you can cover for me, if need be." After zipping up his case, Dakota flopped into the brown leather recliner across from his brother and proceeded to describe what had happened to him a few hours ago, at the diner.

Montana was intrigued. "So, let me get this straight. Elizabeth wants you to meet the family as her husband, because she thinks you're an old-fashioned cowboy."

"Yep. I thought telling her we herd cattle on ATV's these days would only burst her bubble."

"And, she doesn't know that our family is wealthier than hers?"

"No. And I'm not going to tell her. Yet. For now, she knows that I'm the foreman on Big Daddy's ranch. I can tell she thinks I live from paycheck to paycheck. She's never heard of Big Daddy, or our dad, or their oil fields or their companies."

Montana hooted. "What rock has she been living under?"

"Remember, she hates money. From what I gather, she has spent the better part of her life running from anything that smacks of high finance. Says it ruins perfectly good people and turns them into Satan's minions."

Montana grinned. "She sounds too good to be true. She got any sisters? I could probably rustle up a pair of them ugly chaps and woo her."

"I don't know. But if her brother, Charles, is any indication of what the rest of the family is like, I get the feeling that Elizabeth is like that Marilyn character on the Munsters."

"And you're Mr. Marilyn Munster."

Dakota pulled his mouth into a rueful twist. "For the weekend, yes."

When Dakota pulled up to Elizabeth's place in an old flatbed that was covered with dents and gray primer spray, she was delighted. Already packed for the weekend and waiting on the curb, she watched as he maneuvered through the tiny street of the trailer park where she lived. With amazing precision, he turned around in the driveway of her neighbor, old Mr. Breckenridge. Then, after managing to avoid his many yard decorations and flower beds, Dakota pulled to a stop in front of her own humble abode.

When he'd told her that he would come for her in his truck, Elizabeth had never, in her wildest imaginings, thought that he'd arrive in this rolling sludge factory. Thick, black smoke belched from several pipes, both above the cab and beneath the bed, and the engine snarled like a wounded lion. She couldn't wait to see Victoria's face when they pulled up in this. Glee, like champagne bubbles, rose to her throat.

It was perfect.

Though Dakota had cut the engine, the old diesel continued to sputter and shimmy, trying to resurrect itself for a good fifteen seconds after he'd leapt to the ground.

"Ready to go?" His winsome grin, as usual, had her heart leaping into her throat. She pretended not to notice, worried that if she let him see how weak in the knees she went every time he smiled, she might scare him away. She needed him far too much to let that happen.

"As I'll ever be, I guess."

Muscles bulging, he hefted her bags up into the cab of the old rig. As she peered past the door, she noticed how considerate he'd been to spread a lovely Indian print blanket over the soiled black leather upholstery. Several pillows lay over bare springs that protruded through old tears in the seat. A clean scrap of carpet graced the floor, and—though the old girl was obviously used in the dust-laden world of ranching—her interior was devoid of litter. A small fan had been clipped to the passenger-side dash to circulate the air. Even the radio was tuned to the pop station she favored.

Elizabeth nibbled her lower lip. He was such a sweet man. For a moment, she played out the fantasy in her mind that this was real. The cowboy was hers to keep, as was the intense happiness that radiated throughout her body.

He held a hand out to her. "It's kind of high." The sheepish apology in his expression was so endearing. Her heart flip-flopped again and she took pains not to let it show.

She took his hand and murmured, "Thank you."

After boosting her to the running board, his hands slid to her waist and he assisted her up into her seat.

"The seat belt is the lap type. Better put it on and cinch it down tight. This old girl is safe as houses, but you never know." His dimples flashed just before he slammed the door.

She did as he bid, and they were off. They made small talk—Mr. Breckenridge's cluttered garden, her own little place and the fact that she got Valda to sub for her tomorrow—until they hit the highway. They had to talk a little louder than usual to be heard above the noisy *clackity ping* of the engine, but for Elizabeth, that only added to the sense of adventure.

Once Dakota had the old rig up to speed, he settled his lanky frame into a relaxed position for the long haul.

Shadows were lengthening over the rolling terrain between Hidden Valley and Dallas. The sun, a giant tangerine now, shimmered overhead, just beginning its daily descent toward the western horizon. Elizabeth's hands twisted in her lap as she darted a quick glance at Dakota's face. In a few short hours, they would be pulling up to Victoria's as husband and wife. The very idea had her insides pulled tighter than a miser's purse strings. Perhaps a little snack would settle her stomach.

"I took the liberty of having Ned make us some sandwiches because dinner isn't until eight. Hungry?"

"Starved."

Gratified, she smiled. "Good." She rummaged around in the plastic bag she'd brought and pulled out a foil-wrapped lump. "Hope you like smoked turkey and provolone."

"Love it."

He took the sandwich and, steering with his forearms, unwrapped it and took a healthy bite. They talked as they ate.

"You know," she said, lipping a bit of lettuce into her mouth and thoughtfully chewing, "this might be a good time to get our story straight."

"Our story?"

"I thought we might want to be on the same page about how we met and stuff."

"You mean you don't like flying by the seat of your pants the way we did earlier?"

"Not that it wasn't amusing to discover that we'd been married by an Elvis impersonator, but no. My poor nerves can't take it."

Their laughter rumbled along with the engine.

"Okay," he said, draping his wrist over the wheel and letting his hand dangle. "But first, why don't you tell me a little bit about your family. Then I'll tell you about mine, and then we can figure out our own story from there."

"Good idea. Hmm." Elizabeth folded the foil further down around her sandwich. "In order to finish before the turn of the next century, I'll give you the abridged version."

"Okey-dokey." Dakota's interest seemed to be the real article and he leaned toward her in order to catch every word.

The old truck bounced over some ruts in the road, adding to the already ebullient feelings that danced in her stomach. Never had she felt so completely…happy with a person. Even though they came from totally different worlds, she knew that he would understand the complexities of her lifestyle and sympathize. He was amazing that way.

"Ever hear of Lindon House Cosmetics?"

"Can't say that I've used the products." His face lit with easy humor. "But the company name rings a bell. Heard something recently about another stock split, if I'm not mistaken."

"Very good. I'm impressed." She stared at him in surprise, then felt guilty. Just because someone was poor didn't mean they didn't read the paper or watch the news. "Well, Lindon House Cosmetics is one of the largest makeup companies in the world. And my grandmother owns Lindon House Cosmetics. Victoria's great-grandmother started the company in her kitchen over a hundred years ago and it's been passed down from female descendant to female descendant and, since my mother is deceased…"

"It's your turn."

Elizabeth smiled miserably and let her shoulders slump.

"You don't look too thrilled about that."

"It's not the idea of running a company that bothers me, really."

"No?"

"No, it's the wealth."

"The wealth?" Though his tone was deadpan, Dakota winced, and she knew that he must be thinking about his own humble origins.

"Yes." She dabbed at her lips with a paper napkin and hoped that she wasn't going to make him feel self-conscious. But, her wealthy history was a fact that she couldn't sugarcoat. He was going to see it firsthand very shortly. "It's extreme. The kind of disgusting affluence that has had a...shall we say...unbecoming effect on my family. Unfortunately, you'll find out soon enough."

Dakota—eating as he listened—made a noncommittal noise in his throat. When he'd swallowed he suggested, "Tell me about Bernard."

"Bernard Mona is my grandmother's best friend's youngest son. He owns the Monaco's department store chain, which just happens to be Lindon House's biggest customer. A marriage between Bernard and me would be very advantageous to my family's financial situation."

"But you don't love him."

"No. But Victoria wants me to marry him anyway. He's her first pick. I—" she hesitated, wondering how deep this conversation should go, but needing him to see how it was between her and Bernard. "I don't have any desire to get married. I don't know how many ways I can say it to make my family understand. You know what I mean?" When she looked at him to gauge his reaction, he exhaled and rotated his shoulders.

"You don't have any desire to get married. Yes. I think I know what you're saying."

Elizabeth met Dakota's eyes and hoped he got her subtle message. For her, Bernard was out of the picture. She was single, and available.

The thermos she had brought was filled with iced tea. She poured them each a paper cup full, then set them in the plastic holder that protruded from under the dash and, as she refastened the cap, sighed.

"Yes, good old Victoria enjoys playing the matchmaker, although, much to her frustration, without success. My mother was as rebellious as I am and married my father for love. Sadly, I think part of the reason Victoria is so anxious to have me inherit Lindon House is because my own parents passed away before my mother could take over."

"I'm sorry to hear about your parents. That must be rough."

"Mmm. It is. Both my parents were wonderful people, who couldn't have cared less about money. They died when I was a child, in a ferry accident. They'd been doing what they love best, traveling around the world, helping people in need in Third World countries. Someday, I want to be just like them. Right now, I help out on my days off at the Hidden Valley Soup Kitchen. I peel potatoes and mop floors and wash dishes. Victoria would have a cow."

As he tore his gaze from the road to focus on her, the admiration was nearly palpable. "You are really something."

"No. My parents were, though." Feeling suddenly bashful, Elizabeth brought the subject back on track. "Anyway, the rest of my family all lives together at Lindon House, Victoria's mansion, which, obviously, she named after her company. My grandmother wouldn't have it any other way."

As they merged from the highway onto the freeway and headed toward Dallas, Elizabeth went over the pertinent details that any husband would know about her life.

"I have one brother, Charles, whom you have met, and unfortunately, no sisters. Victoria's son, and my mother's thrice-divorced brother, Ashby, lives in the east wing with his fourth wife, Rainbow, a self-named child of the universe, and whichever of Ashby's five hedonistic sons happens to be in the country at the moment, which luckily, isn't often. There are five of us most of the time, but you'd think there were fifty, as noisy as the constant bickering and fighting can get. Even at lunch rush, the Lonestar Grill is a study in tranquillity by comparison."

As they putted down the road, Elizabeth regaled Dakota with tales of her life growing up at Lindon House. She described the acres of landscape, the fleet of rare automobiles, the servants, the pools, the tennis courts and the sharp-edged loneliness that no amount of money could assuage. She told of a childhood spent in a virtual prison of piano and elocution lessons, and how she longed to escape and to laugh and shriek and run and get dirty with the servants' children.

She went on to describe her own suite of rooms in the upper west wing and—though the subject was rather mortifying—she assured him that there were so many rooms that no one would be the wiser if they did not sleep together. He could stay in a connecting room, as long as they made the bed first thing every morning. Certainly, she mused out loud, they could figure out the little married behaviors that would throw the family and servants off their track.

Dakota agreed.

After an hour on the road, the diesel engine was churning along at a comfortable pace that was on target to have them arrive at Victoria's shortly before sunset. The slanting rays of the lowering sun warmed the interior of the cab, bringing forth the smells of dirty rubber and motor oil long ago spilled beneath their feet. They were both grateful for the little fan clipped to the dash.

Eyes off the road, Dakota glanced sideways at her for an instant.

"Anybody else I should know about?"

"There are a dozen servants running around all the time, but due to the less than pleasant working conditions, they tend to quit on a regular basis. I probably won't even recognize half of them." She gestured loosely at him with what was left of her sandwich. "You're pretty much up to speed on my life. Why don't you tell me about yours?"

There was a longing quality in her inflection that had Dakota glancing at her again. He reached for his cup of iced tea and wondered how to tell the story of his family without bringing up the issue of money. He took a long pull on his drink. Money didn't corrupt all families. His own father and uncle were living testament to that fact. However, he figured it might be best if he just continued to omit that part of the history for now.

"Well, I come from a pretty big family. It's not too hard keeping 'em all straight, if you just remember that my father's older brother, is a huge fan of country music. My uncle, Big Daddy Brubaker, has nine kids, all named after country-and-western singers."

Elizabeth's lilting laughter made him smile. "You're kidding."

"Nope. There's Conway, Merle, Buck, Patsy, Johnny, Kenny, the twins, Waylon and Willie and Hank."

"Wow," Elizabeth murmured and Dakota could see her matching each name to a famous singer in her mind's eye. "Big Daddy is the one who owns the ranch where you work, right?"

"Right. Before each of us is allowed to take a job with the family business, we help him run the ranch for a while."

Elizabeth took a breath and opened her mouth to speak, but he forged ahead, not wanting to give her time to ask about the family business. "My dad is Tiny Brubaker."

"Tiny?" Again, Elizabeth's laughter warmed him, causing a chuckle to rumble in his own throat.

"Yeah, he was nicknamed Tiny because he is well over six feet."

"If that's tiny, how big is Big Daddy?"

"Comes up to 'bout here," Dakota gestured to his bicep, "on me."

The casual lift of her shoulder said "whatever" and grinning, she nodded for him to go on.

"Anyway, Dad and my mother, Bernice, also have nine kids. I'm the oldest. When it came to naming us, my dad was just as creative as his brother."

"Let me guess." Elizabeth held up a palm. "Alex, I'll take people who are named after states for a thousand."

"You are good." It seemed impossible, but he liked her more with every passing mile. "My dad is probably the most patriotic man you'll ever want to meet and so that would explain the names. Anyhow, there are four boys. Me, Montana, Tex, and Kentucky who goes by Tucker. There are five girls. Virginia, who everyone calls Ginny, then there is Carolina, Georgia, Maryland, who goes by Mary and last but not least little Louise-Anna. She's still in high school."

"Where do they live?"

"Montana shares a bunkhouse with me. The rest of 'em live at home. We have a place, not too far from the Circle BO, but we don't run cattle out there." There were too many oil rigs to run cattle, but Dakota figured that was beside the point.

"And you've never been married?"

Dakota flexed his hands on the steering wheel. "Nah. Like you, I've just never met the right person." *Until now,* he wanted to shout, but instead, decided to lean back and play it cool. Didn't want to scare her off with his interest. He yawned, just for effect. "I'm not ready to settle down yet either. Maybe someday, but definitely not now."

"Oh."

He glanced askance at her, to see how she was reacting,

and she seemed pleased with this announcement if her bright smile was any indication.

"Anyhow, those are most of the pertinent details about my life. So, what's *our* story, babe?"

"Our story." Her eyes were glassy.

"Yeah. Remember, you wanted us to come up with a story. When did you first fall in love with me, when did I first fall in love with you, how did I propose, you know, all the little things we should know about each other."

"Oh, right. Of course. I'm sorry, I was zoning out there, for a minute." She ducked her head into the large lunch bag, and pulled out a plastic Baggie. "Chips?"

"Sure." Intentionally brushing her fingers with his, he took the bag, but longed to take her hand instead. "So, when did you first fall for me?"

"I, well, let's see. Let's tell them that I, uh, fell in love with you the third time you came in to have lunch on my shift. The first time you came in, all the women in the place noticed and I wondered what was up with that."

Dakota rolled his eyes. Those women all knew of his financial standings, hence most of the interest. "And, so what did you decide was up with that?"

"Well, for one thing, you are...er...gorgeous."

He made a disparaging sound.

"Come on. It's true and you know it. The second time you came in, I noticed how genuinely nice you were. And, by the third time you came in, I was head over heels for you."

"That," Dakota withheld a wishful sigh, "sounds good. For me, on the other hand, it was love at first sight. I'll just stick to the story I told Charles about wanting to kiss you from the beginning."

"Uh, okay." Again, she ducked into the bag. "Cookie?"

"Okay."

She tossed him another foil packet. "Chocolate chip."

"Thanks. When did I propose?"

"I don't know. It should be romantic, though."

"How about if we tell them I took you out to the ranch and we went horseback riding, because I knew you loved horses and had every horse book a little girl could want."

She darted a sharp, searching look at him. She was surprised that he'd remember that about her.

"And we had a picnic under the stars, and I got down on bended knee and begged you to be my wife and the mother of our little daughters, who would look just like you, of course, and I kissed you, right here...."

He took his eyes off the road just long enough to touch her lips with his forefinger.

"Uh, okay. That..." she closed her eyes and took a deep breath, "...that sounds perfect."

To Elizabeth, the miles seemed to melt away as they organized the strategy that would get them through the next few days. For the most part, their camaraderie was easy. Yet, every so often their gazes would collide and hold for an extra beat. Embarrassed, she would look away and pretend that the electricity that sparked between them didn't really exist. Dakota had made it clear that he was not ready for any kind of commitment, he was simply doing her a favor. As she stuffed her disappointment to the deep recesses of her soul, she knew that she'd do well to keep that in mind.

Before either of them could believe it, they'd reached the Dallas city limits. Victoria's massive estate was situated on a hill overlooking the city, in a sprawling area that reeked of money. In the waning twilight, Elizabeth navigated as Dakota drove them through the cobbled streets, where the sidewalks were surrounded by perfectly trimmed box hedges and lush flowering vegetation. Overhead, streetlights were beginning to buzz on and the citrus-colored sunset was giving way to a light violet.

Elizabeth studied Dakota's profile and wondered how he was faring. A neighborhood like this could intimidate even those who lived there. Even so, his body language declared that he was at ease driving his rickety rig through some of the country's finest real estate. She tore her gaze from his face and planted it on the road. There was nothing more appealing than a man who was confident in his own skin.

Before she'd decided to ask Dakota to come home with her for the weekend she'd considered his strengths and knew that he was not one that Victoria could easily cow. Just knowing that infused her with a sense of calm.

"Right up here, at this circular intersection…"

"Yeah?"

"Take a right. Then, go up to the top of the rise in the road there, and you'll see the gates. Just pull up to the brick post and we can punch in the code."

"Gottcha."

After the iron gates swung open, Dakota drove down the long, tree-lined driveway with the confidence of a man who might be driving a Jaguar. In the front of the rambling Tudor style mansion, where the drive turned circular, a beautifully lit fountain shot a stair-stepping stream straight into the air. There, it hovered at the apex before cascading into a koi filled pool. Giant twin lions carved from marble flanked the front steps and inside the house, the lights were ablaze.

As Dakota pulled to a stop under the portico and did his level best to kill the engine, the impressive front doors swung open and a butler that Elizabeth did not recognize, rushed to send them packing.

Ignoring the butler's flustered admonitions, Dakota shoved open his door and jumping to the shiny aggregate drive, rounded the front of the truck and opened Elizabeth's door for her. He swung her into his arms and she was headed with him toward the mansion's massive steps when the butler caught up with them.

"I'm afraid you can't park that…that…thing here, sir. You'll need an appointment in order to visit here," he brandished his clipboard, "and I do not see where you are listed…"

From behind the leaded glass panes of the mahogany sidelights that flanked the front doors, a hacking cough sounded.

"Simon?" The feeble voice carried out toward the portico.

The butler spun on his heels. "Yes, ma'am?"

"Who is there?"

Elizabeth sighed. "It's me, Grandmother."

"Elizabeth? Is that you?" The wizened voice cracked, then fell into another coughing fit.

"Yes. Me…and," she shot Dakota a do-or-die look, "my husband."

Silence fell.

The butler, new since Elizabeth had left, stared, open-mouthed.

Elizabeth turned her back on the house, and smiling up at Dakota whispered, "Sorry to put you on the spot this way, but she's watching us like a hawk. Now would be a good time to do something husbandly like…" she tapped her cheek with her forefinger, "kiss me."

Chapter Four

Elizabeth strained toward Dakota on tiptoe, lifting her cheek to his mouth for a little peck that she hoped would demonstrate their solidarity to Victoria. Deliberately or not—she'd never know for sure—Dakota misinterpreted the offer of her cheek. When she'd suggested that he kiss her, she hadn't expected that he'd respond with such...gusto. It took her completely off guard.

With strong, capable hands he cupped her face and, drawing her near, whispered, "Sure. No problem."

Before she could protest that a simple gesture would do, he lowered his lips to hers. The kiss started off soft and unhurried and built in intensity as he coaxed a response from her that—much to her chagrin—she gave, in spite of herself. In rhythm with his, her breathing quickened. As his mouth moved over hers, the pads of his thumbs traced the line of her jaw, the sensitive spots at the sides of her neck and then, the hollow of her throat. Legs tingling and shaky, she circled his slim waist with her arms and clung to him in order to keep from slipping to the ground.

Even in this muzzy state of mind, Elizabeth was summarily impressed by how believably he played his role. In order to convince Victoria that she was his, Dakota was making quite the show of staking his claim. Even knowing it was simply part of the plan, she thrilled to the possession in his touch.

"There. That ought to make some kind of impression," he murmured against her lips. His hair brushed her cheek as he broke their kiss and nuzzled her neck with his nose.

"Oh, my. Yes, I'm sure it, uh, made an impression." Her whisper sounded breathless and squeaky to her ears.

Elizabeth took a step back and attempted to pull herself together. Her grandmother was watching. She needed to act as if this was an everyday occurrence. As if they kissed this way all the time. She needed to appear blasé. Nonchalant. She could do this. She had to. Her future and her sanity depended on it.

"Come on, honey, I want you to meet my grandmother," she called gaily, as if she didn't really feel the nervous tick that chose that moment to settle in her eye.

"I can't wait, sweetheart," he lifted his voice for Victoria's benefit, then whispered out of the side of his mouth, "how am I doing?"

"Great." She swallowed and glanced toward the house. She could make out Victoria's frail outline, hovering beyond the door. "In fact, after that display, *I* almost believe we are married."

The cocky grin she'd come to admire stole across his face, deepening his dimples. "I aim to give you your money's worth."

"Gee. Thanks." Of course. It was always about money, was it not? He was simply a hired hand, doing a job. She must remember that. After all, she'd been raised in a home where money always bought love and affection. Eye twitching crazily, at the prospect of facing Victoria, Elizabeth sighed.

Mistaking her intention, Dakota returned her eye spasm with a roguish wink of his own, then flung an arm over her shoulders. As he propelled her toward the butler, he dug a mangled dollar bill from the wallet in his hip pocket and pressed it into Simon's hand.

"The keys are in the ignition, buddy. Good luck. She's got a tricky clutch."

Simon stared with distaste, first at the bill in his hand, then at the truck. Finally, resigning himself to the task, he climbed into the cab and after a few noisy false starts, fired up the engine.

From the shadowed foyer, Victoria emerged dragging an oxygen tank on tiny wheels behind her and sucking air from the mask. Her supreme censure was unmistakable as she watched Simon grind through the flatbed's gearbox, searching for the one that would set him in motion.

Elizabeth clutched Dakota's arm and they mounted and climbed the stairs together. This was going to be a little tougher than she'd originally thought.

Victoria was an imposing woman, in spite of the fact that now that she'd reached her eighties, she'd shrunk considerably from her original statuesque height. The years had taken their toll and her shoulders were stooped, and her still shapely legs, somewhat bowed. Her platinum blond hair was swept up in a regal fashion to the crown of her head. Though her once flawless complexion was now tissue paper thin and covered with lines, her aristocratic bone structure was still evident and it was easy to see that she'd been stunning in her youth. Crimson lips pursed, false lashes fluttering behind her trifocals, her gaze narrowed at Dakota.

"Who is he?" Victoria demanded.

Elizabeth glanced at Dakota. "Charles didn't tell you?"

"Tell me what?"

"That I was bringing my...my...husband with me to meet the family."

"Yes, he told me that, but I didn't believe him," Victoria snapped.

With a deep, fortifying breath, Elizabeth rubbed the muscle that jumped in her eye and plunged ahead. "Grandmother, I'd, uh, like to introduce...ah, hem, I want you to meet—"

Dakota stepped forward and held out his hand. "Dakota Brubaker. I run the ranch out at the Circle BO, it's a little spread just outside of Hidden Valley." When Victoria ignored his outstretched hand, he clasped them together. "I have to say that this is a real treat. I've sure been looking forward to meeting my Little Bit's Nanna. She's told me so much about you. It's a real privilege to be part of your family, ma'am."

Victoria let go of the handle to her tank so that she could clutch her chest. The tank clanked to the floor. "Simon, Simon! My pills! My wheelchair!"

Unfortunately, Simon was not able to hear her pleas over the lurchings and skiddings of Dakota's truck as he moved from the portico to the parking area near the massive, two-story garage.

"Grandmother?" Elizabeth looked helplessly at Dakota.

Nodding at Elizabeth to grab the oxygen tank, Dakota swept the tiny woman into his arms. He shot her a "where-to" look, as Victoria suddenly revived and began to protest much more loudly than her condition would indicate her capable.

"In there." Elizabeth pointed to a set of floor-to-ceiling doors off the foyer and to the left of the curved staircase.

"Put me down this instant, you...you...plebeian upstart!'' Victoria struggled against them as together, they ushered her into the elegant front parlor. She whapped Dakota upside the head with a surprising strength that had him wincing in pain.

"Now, Nanna, you shouldn't be carrying on this way. You need to save your strength," he admonished and settled the featherlight matriarch into a chair near the fireplace.

"Stop calling me that horrible name, you nincompoop."

Any fears that Elizabeth had harbored about damaging Victoria by announcing her marriage to Dakota vanished. The old bird was as feisty as a bantam rooster.

Elizabeth took the chair opposite Victoria and studied her for a moment. "Are you going to be all right, Grandmother?"

"Of course I'm *not* all right," Victoria groused. She clapped the oxygen mask over her mouth and sucked deeply, then jerked it away. "Elizabeth, is this…*marriage* another one of your scalawag schemes to get me off your back about taking over the company and marrying Bernard? Charles seems to think so." She shot a scathing look at Dakota as he moved to stand behind Elizabeth. "If it is, I can tell you right now, it's not going to work."

Elizabeth schooled her face into a mask of innocence and looked wide-eyed at Dakota. "Scheme?"

He shrugged. "What's she talking about, sugar lips?"

The pet name, though silly, reminded her of his kiss and she shivered in her seat. "I have no idea."

"Don't play dumb with me, missy. I know you are up to something."

"You do?" Elizabeth fingered the tubing to the oxygen tank. "Shouldn't you be in bed? I hear you're not long for this world."

"This time, it's true." Victoria batted Elizabeth's hand

away from her equipment. "So. I take it that this—" she fluttered her fingers in a dismissive manner at Dakota, "—means I should call off the engagement party I've been planning for you and Bernard?"

"I don't think that plannin' an engagement party for *my* Little Bit would be such a good idea." Though Dakota's tone was droll, something about his expression said that he was not entirely amused.

Victoria glared at him.

"An engagement party for me and Bernard? Oh, Grandmother, please." Exasperated, Elizabeth exhaled, long and slow. "Apparently my breaking off with Bernard and telling him that I never loved him and never would, hasn't put a damper on our future in your mind. Why on earth would you be planning a party? I thought you were deathly ill."

As if suddenly remembering that this were the case, Victoria fell into a dramatic coughing fit. "I tell you I am!" she moaned when she could speak again. "Can you think of a better time to throw a party for my only granddaughter and heir to my fortune?" At the mention of her assets, she cast her suspicious gaze upon Dakota. "Perhaps you would prefer to wait until after I'm dead, and can't come?"

"Don't be ridiculous."

Disheveled from his traumatic parking experience, Simon arrived in the parlor with their bags.

"Where would you like these, ma'am?"

Victoria looked back and forth between the two of them for a long moment, as if weighing the validity of their union. She heaved a sigh of resignation. "Take them to Elizabeth's suite."

Dakota leapt to his feet and offered another dollar to the harried servant. Simon stared at the bill, then after a beat said dryly, "Mrs. Derovencourt handles my gratuity."

"Well, now, that may," he raised a skeptical brow, "—or may not be true, but I pay my own way around here." Dakota tucked the ratty dollar bill in Simon's shirt pocket and patted his chest. "There you go, buddy boy. Just put our things in the little woman's room."

Elizabeth smiled, admiring his strong sense of self, even in these rather daunting surroundings.

"As you wish, sir."

The clock on the mantle delicately chimed the half hour.

Victoria glanced at the diamond studded watch on her wrist. "Dinner will be served in the dining room at eight. The entire family will be there, and they are all looking forward to seeing you, Elizabeth." She made a point of ignoring Dakota. "Everyone is dressing for the occasion as we speak. May I suggest that you retire to your room and do the same?"

Dakota glanced down at his clothes, then to Elizabeth. "I'm already dressed, L.B." He smiled at Victoria and ran his hands over the broad muscles of his chest. "This is my best shirt."

Victoria closed her eyes and took a deep drag from the oxygen mask. "He looks to be about Charles's size. I'll have something delivered."

"Well, here we are. Home sweet home." After Simon had delivered their luggage and beat a hasty retreat, Elizabeth closed her bedroom doors and turned to face Dakota.

He tossed their bags on the floor and looked around. The magnificent suite was as big as his bunkhouse, and was pretty much on par with anything his family owned in terms of elegance and taste. He felt completely at home, having grown up in similar digs, himself. "This was your room?"

"Yes, come on, I'll show you around." Elizabeth

grasped him by the hand and took him on a mini tour of the place where she'd spent her formative years. "This is the sitting room, and through this archway, is my bedroom and the master bath." The clicking of their heels echoed on the marble floor as they strolled from the opulent bath through the giant walk-in closet. From there, they traveled to the hall that led to the guest bedroom and bath. Elizabeth swept an arm around the room that was to be his. "I hope you'll be comfortable in here."

"It sure beats the bunkhouse."

Elizabeth's smile was wan. "I wouldn't be so sure about that. The bunkhouse sounds like a lot of laughs."

"It is."

"We'll have to be sure to get up early and make the bed in the morning, so that the maids don't catch on that we're not..." she averted her eyes, "you know. Gossip spreads like the common cold around here."

Dakota's gaze lingered on the bed. They wouldn't have that dilemma, if they were really married. They'd be snuggled up in the same bed, like spoons, and wouldn't have to worry about what the maids thought. But, from what she'd said about Bernard earlier, marriage was the furthest thing from her mind. Maybe, if things went well this weekend, he could begin to change all that. He was sure going to try.

The moment grew awkward as they gazed at his bed, each lost in private thought. Their eyes collided for an electric beat, and then, growing self-conscious they smiled. Dakota groped for something to say that would ease the tension. Luckily, a knock sounded at the door. Elizabeth sprang to see who was there.

Simon stood in the hallway, carrying one of Charles's dress suits.

"I got it, lambchop," Dakota said, coming to step between her and the door. Once again, he dug a dollar from his pocket, thrust it at Simon and got a charge out of the way the stuffy butler bristled like a blowfish. Playing the part of Elizabeth's hayseed husband was the most fun he'd had in ages. He took the suit, handed it to Elizabeth and closed the door in Simon's face.

"So," he said when they were alone again, "how do you think your plan is working so far?"

"I don't really know. It's so hard to tell with Victoria sometimes. She didn't react as badly as I'd hoped."

"She seemed pretty shocked to me."

"Shocked, yes, but she hasn't kicked us out yet. That's the goal. If we stay the course, I think we'll get there. I wonder what she's planning," Elizabeth mused as she tugged the plastic off Charles's suit. "I just hope she doesn't end up taking a shine to you."

Victoria's glacial glare loomed in his mind's eye. "I don't think there's any danger of that."

"Well, we've made a good start." She stuffed the plastic into a wastebasket and folded the suit over her arm. "But I think we need to kick it up a notch. The countrified cowboy angle is a good one, we just need to play it up a little more. You need to act like more of a hick. A hillbilly goofy-doof. You know what I mean."

Dakota looped his thumbs through his belt loops and rocked back on his heels. "Aw, shucks, Little Bit, I love it when you sweet-talk me like 'at."

"Excellent. Nice touch with the nickname, too. Victoria hates those." An impish grin on her face, Dakota could see the wheels turning in her gorgeous head. "And, maybe you need to come across as more possessive. The more controlling of me you are, the better. If Victoria thinks that her precious company would end up at the mercy of someone who doesn't have a clue, there is no way she'll give it to me."

"And that makes you happy?"

"Ecstatic."

For a moment, Dakota wondered what his family would say if he denounced his fortune for the woman he loved. They'd think he was nuts, but they'd no doubt be supportive and loving.

"And, um, there's one other thing," she looked up at him, seeming suddenly flustered. Nervously, she plucked a stray thread off the suit. "I, uh, I think we should strive to appear as if we are, you know, sort of er, hot, for each other." She hastened to explain. "I don't want Victoria to think that there would be any backing out of this marriage for me. That's very important."

Dakota battled back the wave of excitement he felt at her suggestion and struggled to appear cool. "No problem. I can do that."

"I'm…sure you can." She hid her flaming face behind Charles's suit as she held it out to him. "Here. Put this on. I'll change in my closet."

He unbuttoned his shirt and stripped it off as Elizabeth disappeared into the next room. The soft rustlings of fabric puddling to the floor had his libido working overtime. *She was taking her clothes off in there.* The thought had him fumbling with the buttons to Charles's dress shirt. He needed to focus on the task at hand, if he was going to make it through this weekend with his mind, not to mention his heart, in one piece.

Her muffled voice reached him from the closet. "Dakota?"

"Yeah?"

"I think I should warn you that my family argues a lot."

"You mentioned that."

"Yes, well, it's the kind of thing you have to see to believe."

"I can handle it."

There was a smile in her voice. "Okay."

His own family had been known to argue a time or two. Get twenty or thirty Brubaker cousins around the dining room table at Thanksgiving, and the arguments were bound to happen. But they'd blow over as easily as they'd flare. His dad would see to that. There was nothing more important to Tiny Brubaker than family love. And, he made sure his offspring understood that. Even if he had to crack their heads together to get the point across.

Within moments of his finishing dressing, Elizabeth emerged. She looking like a vision in a slinky black cocktail dress that clung to her wonderful figure like ivy to a brick wall. His throat closed. She was incredible.

She stopped and stared at him, her lips forming a soft *O,* her eyes going glassy. "Oh, dear. This..." she swallowed, and indicated his suit, "this will never do."

He tugged at the jacket. "Yeah, I know. I'm a little broader than Chuck, through the shoulders, but it will probably be okay if I don't get too active and go like—" He raised his arms over his head.

"No, it's not that. You look too," she touched her tongue to her lips, "well, you look too urbane. Too Double-O-Seven."

Feeling self-conscious, he looked down at himself. "I do?"

Elizabeth sighed. "Yes. My family won't hate you quite as much, the way you're dressed now."

"Well, that's no good." He grinned at the irony. "Hmm. Wait. I have something that might help." In two long strides, he reached the couch and unzipped his duffel bag. "What do you think of this?" he asked, and held up the silver belt buckle that weighed five pounds, if it weighed an ounce.

She clapped her hands and laughed out loud. "I love it. Put it on!" Peering into the bag she asked, "What else have you got in there?"

For the next few minutes their mirth filled the room as they pored over the accessories that Dakota had pulled from his rodeo keepsake trunk.

"Here," he tossed a pair of cowboy boots on the floor. "These were my cousin, Patsy's. She loaned me these and some other stuff for you. You're about her size. Thought they might make a cool addition to your outfit."

Elizabeth hiked her skirt and slipped her feet into the boots. They were a bit snug in the toe, but that wouldn't matter, being that they were just walking to the table. "Ooo. Gotta love this look." Toe to floor, she swiveled her ankle back and forth, her gaze admiring.

He smiled. "Too bad you were born in the city, because you make a real natural looking cowgirl."

"You think?"

"Yep." Next, he dug out the chaps.

"Oh, you've gotta wear those! They're so horrible," she crowed, and traced the colorful engraving with her fingertips.

"Horrible? Hey now, I wore these in my first rodeo. The girls all loved 'em. Practically tore 'em off me."

"That, I can believe. What events were you in?"

"Back then? Bull riding."

"You're kidding."

"No. I was nuts in those days. Those bad boys grow to be as big as freight trains. Freight trains with attitude. See this mark here?" He rubbed his fingertip over a gouge that ran from the top of one chap, to the middle.

Elizabeth nodded. "Um-hum."

"These ugly chaps probably saved my leg."

"How?"

"Ol' bull didn't like bein' rode."

"He gored you?" Elizabeth gasped and looked at him in horror.

"Tried." He tilted his head. "Rodeo clown dragged me into a barrel. Saved my sorry behind that day."

"Oh my gosh! You don't do that anymore, do you?"

"Nah. I'm too old."

"You're not too old."

"My back is." With a rueful grin, Dakota tossed the wild chaps on the couch. "Anyway, it's tempting to wear these tonight, but don't you think they're just a little too much? Nanna would know we're puttin' her on, if I show up in these. Let's save these for a less formal occasion."

She pouted. "Yeah, you're probably right. Darn."

"How about this?" He clapped his Stetson on and adjusted the brim to the perfect angle, just above his eyes.

"Love it."

"Good, because I brought one for you, too." He dug it out and balanced it on her silky, gold hair. She beamed and he thought he'd never seen anyone look so beautiful. "That looks good with the boots."

"You're so smart to think of bringing this stuff."

"Shucks, now, honey. You're givin' me a big head." A bashful grin on his face, he rummaged some more in his bag, withdrew the spurs and pushed them onto the heels of his cowboy boots. "These would make a nice statement, don't you think? They jangle real purty when I walk."

Elizabeth angled her head and eyes glowing, nodded. "Perfect."

"And you can wear my blue ribbon." He drew her toward him and his hands shook as he carefully pinned the gaudy, ruffly award just above her bosom. "Because you're my first prize.'' A dreamy sigh escaped her lips, causing his fumbling to increase.

"I'm honored.''

In spite of his nerves, he managed to secure the ribbon's pin to her dress without incident. "Just a sec. We're not done.''

"There's more?''

"One more thing.'' Dakota unzipped a pocket inside his bag and unearthed a tiny box that he'd thought to pack at the last minute. "This belonged to my great-grand-mother,'' he said, feeling suddenly shy. At home, it had seemed like such a good idea. What if she didn't like it?

He needn't have worried.

Elizabeth opened the box, and her expression grew soft and her eyes, dewy. A soft sigh escaped her lips. With awe, she extracted the simple wedding set with silver fili-gree and a tiny quarter-carat diamond. "It's so beautiful,'' she breathed, her eyes glowing. "Are you sure you want me to wear it?''

"I can't think of anyone I'd rather have wear this, than you,'' he said, and meant it more than she would ever know. He took the ring from her and held it between the thumb and forefinger of his right hand. In his left hand, he supported her left ring finger and their gazes tangled and danced. "Elizabeth Derovencourt, will you marry me?''

Her breath caught, and she blinked at him, stunned. "I…I…'' she smiled and laughed. "Yes!''

Even though it wasn't a real proposal, and her response wasn't a real acceptance, Dakota felt a powerful sense of awe. Gently, he slipped the ring on her finger. The fit was perfect, almost as if it had been made for her. The stone and setting were small, but it was surprisingly charming on her slender finger.

"I promise to love, honor and cherish you till the end of our days together." He tugged her forward and brushed his lips lightly against hers in a kiss that almost wasn't.

Her sweet, warm sigh filled his mouth. "I do, too."

"I now pronounce us man and wife." This time, he settled his lips over hers a little more firmly. Then, before he could give in to his baser instincts, he broke the kiss. It would be better not to push things. Might scare her off. She was under the impression that she didn't want a serious commitment. It was up to him to prove her wrong.

The centuries old grandfather clock at the end of the upstairs hall chimed eight.

Dakota rested his forehead against hers. "Time to face the music, wife. You ready?"

Her head bobbed. "As I'll ever be."

As they descended the grand staircase, Elizabeth could hear the nightly bickering already in full swing. Angry voices reverberated, bouncing from arched ceiling to marble floor in a never-ending cacophony of sarcasm.

"See what I mean?" she whispered, clutching Dakota's hand as the memories of her miserable youth came flooding back.

He gave her hand a reassuring squeeze and nodded.

She and Dakota paused in the foyer, just outside the entrance to the formal dining room and listened. Shame tinged her cheeks pink. In a way, it was lucky she was Dakota's employer. The only way she'd ever consider bringing a poor unsuspecting man into this war zone was to pay him.

The voices of her family were already beginning to escalate, and the first course had yet to be completed.

"—I've said it once and I'll say it again. We should simply demand that if it is indeed a real marriage, she have it annulled. It should be obvious to all of us that he only married her for her money. Poor, darling Elizabeth.''

Victoria snorted. ''Don't give me that concerned uncle routine, Ashby. You are simply worried that if Elizabeth doesn't inherit, I'll do as I've been threatening and give control of the company to someone outside the family, and you'll all end up destitute.''

Ashby's tone was brittle. ''That's not it at all, Mother.''

''He's *right,* Victoria. We *care* about Elizabeth.''

''You care about keeping yourselves in caviar, and blue-chip stocks, Rainbow.''

''I *detest* caviar. I *don't* eat *animal* protein.''

Ashby wondered aloud, ''Does anyone know anything about this Brubaker character?''

''Only that he works as a ranch hand on some little spread called the Circle BO,'' Charles put in.

''B…O? What could that mean?'' Rainbow wondered.

Ashby snorted. ''It means something *stinks* about this whole marriage deal, Rainbow. Our niece has tied the knot with a gold-digging gigolo.''

Tone dry, Charles said, ''Much the way her own uncle did.''

Ashby sputtered. ''That's rich, Charles. I'm not the one who skimmed the funds off the top of my best client's account, and then ran off to Switzerland with his wife.''

''Never going to let me live that down, are you, Ashby? As if you've never made a mistake before. Never dallied with another man's…assets. My last fiancée mentioned your wandering eyes.''

Rainbow made a sound of disgust. ''And you'd believe Sophia?''

''At least she never killed anyone out of jealousy.'' Charles sniffed.

''*That* was an *accident!*''

"We've been over this before. Rainbow, you know you shouldn't drink and cook."

Ignoring their spat, Ashby heaved a wounded sigh. "Mother, if you would simply let myself or Charles run the company we wouldn't have to worry about losing control."

"No, instead we'd have to worry about finding it siphoned into a Swiss bank account—"

Charles cleared his throat. "Where is Elizabeth? I thought she and her gold-digging gigolo would have been down here by now."

Dakota glanced down at Elizabeth. How had such a sweet woman emerged from such a despicable family? It was no small wonder she wanted out. More than ever, he was motivated to help.

"Ready?" he whispered, framing her face in his hands and looking deeply into her eyes.

"For what?"

"To get kicked out of the family?"

"Yes." Her sigh was rapturous.

"We have our work cut out for us."

Her eyes had glazed over. "We do?"

"Well, I think it's gonna be tough to out-strange your family."

"True. We'll just have to be creative."

"Okay then. Put your arms around my neck." When she did, Dakota swept her off her feet and up against his chest. Her gasp had him grinning. "Now, Mrs. Brubaker, let's go get thrown out on our ears."

Elizabeth giggled. "I love you, Mr. Brubaker."

Though she may not mean them, her words exhilarated him and he burst through the grand archway into the caveernous dining room, with Elizabeth in his arms. Silence suddenly reigned as all eyes swiveled to the doorway. Jaws dropped and soupspoons froze midair.

Dakota was the first to break the silence.

"Hey, everyone, sorry we're late, but we got into a wrastlin' match up on that old king-size bed of hers, and forgot the time. Where should we sit, darlin'?"

"Put her down," Victoria barked, and brandished her oxygen mask at them. "What is it with you and your caveman need to carry everyone around?" She hacked and wheezed in a most impressive manner and fiddled with the valve on her oxygen tank.

"I guess life with my Little Bit is like one big honeymoon, and every doorway a threshold to our new life."

"Oh, honey. That's so sweet."

A man Dakota figured must be Elizabeth's uncle Ashby was the first to pull himself together. "Elizabeth, darling! Look everyone. It's Elizabeth. And…" his brittle gaze focused upon Dakota. "Her…and, her—"

The faces of Elizabeth's family were suddenly transformed into expressions of pseudo-enthusiasm. Dakota noticed that their eyes seemed to be devoid of any real love or warmth toward the object of their interest.

"Elizabeth!" they burbled, choosing to ignore Dakota and glancing back and forth amongst each other. "You're back!"

"Hello, Uncle Ashby. Rainbow." She waved from the safety of his embrace.

"Elizabeth, darling." Rainbow's eyes landed with dismay on the tiny diamond that adorned her stepniece's ring finger. "We heard that you'd…eloped."

Dakota nodded. "You heard right, ma'am."

"You might have let your family know," Ashby groused.

"Sorry, Uncle Ashby."

Dakota carried Elizabeth over to her aunt and uncle and shifting her in his arms, extended his hand. "Pleased to meetcha, ma'am." He swung Elizabeth around, upsetting Rainbow's place setting with her boots and knocking into her uncle as he did so. "You too, sir. I'm Dakota Brubaker. I run the ranch out at the Circle BO. I just want you to know that I love your niece and intend to do right by her. When I first laid eyes on her, I thought to myself, Dakota old boy, one of the little silver gals on your truck's mud-flaps has sprung to life. All them mushy country songs suddenly started to make sense. Like the one that goes," he began to sing, "I had twenty-twenty vision till I met my little forty-twenty-forty Carolina Honey, now I'm half blind with love and runnin' outta money…" He let his voice trail off and paused to reflect. "You know that song never made a lick of sense to me, till I met Little Bit, here."

Rainbow picked up a cloth napkin and began to fan her-self.

"We were sure sorry we couldn't invite y'all to the wed-din', but it was a small, private affair." He bounced Eliz-abeth a little higher against his chest.

"Just Elvis and us," Elizabeth said in a strangled man-ner. Hat askew, she buried her face into his neck. From the way her shoulders bobbed, he suspected she was laugh-ing. To cover, he emitted an amorous growl.

Furtive peeks from her family made note of their odd attire, and they exchanged loaded glances.

"Sit down," Victoria demanded from the head of the long, formally set dining table, and indicated the two va-cant seats to her right. "Your soup is getting cold."

"Nuthin' worse than cold soup," Dakota announced and let Elizabeth slide down his body till her boots touched the floor. "Unless it's cold possum. *Nuthin'* worse than cold possum. Right, sugar pie?"

Elizabeth took a deep breath. "Right," she agreed, when she'd composed herself and took her seat.

"So," Elizabeth's uncle Ashby began, "Brubaker, why don't you tell us something about yourself."

Spoons clinked as the family observed a brief moratorium on the usual frenzy of sarcasm and sipped with euphonious grace at their soup.

Dakota slurped at his with all the manners of a golden retriever. "Well, like I said, I work on a cattle ranch near Hidden Valley. The Circle BO. When I'm not workin' I try to spend as much time in town with Little Bit as I can. Me and L.B. eat lunch together every day up at Ned's. It's the highlight of my day." Her probing gaze swung to his and he winked. It was true.

"Ned's?" Rainbow's query was polite, but she looked as if she'd been sucking a lemon.

"Lonestar Grill. Where L.B. works. Best half-pound burgers in Texas. Grease everywhere. You'd love 'em. Everybody does."

Rainbow made a choking sound.

Ashby leaned forward, his expression grim. "You'll forgive me if this question seems out of line, but I imagine you can't make much money working on a...cattle ranch."

"Oh, you'd be surprised." Dakota grinned at the humor in this assumption. "Up at the ranch, we have our own bunk and everything. Someday, I hope to build Elizabeth her dream house."

A faraway look crossed Elizabeth's face. "A little cottage with a picket fence, and maybe some land."

"Gotta have some land for that big old passel of kids we're gonna have." Dakota framed Elizabeth's face in his hands and gazed deeply into her eyes.

She leaned toward him, her sigh tickling his lips. "Lots and lots of kids."

His mouth brushed hers as he spoke. "They will need a place to play."

Elizabeth dropped her spoon with a clatter into the china soup bowl and wound her arms around his neck. The slightest pressure from his hands brought her lips full against his, and he kissed her the way he'd always dreamed about, at the diner.

"Kids?" Victoria reached for her oxygen mask, and this time, from the paleness in her cheeks, it looked as if she really needed it.

Dakota tore his mouth from Elizabeth's long enough to say, "At least nine, like my own mama and daddy had."

"All named for states of the union," Elizabeth added. "There's California and Washington, Idaho and Nebraska, Ohio and Florida, Indiana and Kansas and of course, my Dakota."

Rolling with the punches, Dakota shrugged and nodded. "That's the whole fan damnily."

"Nine kids?" Victoria looked positively green.

"Why not?" Dakota wondered and nibbled between sentences at Elizabeth's lips. "I don't believe that a woman should have to work outside the house, if she don't want to. My mama never did, and she was up to her eyeballs with stuff to do. We will be poor, but we will be happy."

A blissful sigh came from Elizabeth. She loved this idea, and only wished Dakota were describing her real future.

"Elizabeth, as head of this family and the voice of reason, I demand that you have this…this…prison sentence annulled. Immediately!"

"Annulled?" Wounded, Dakota stared at Victoria, then at Elizabeth. She could tell by the muscle that jumped in his jaw that he was really warming up to his role. "Oh, no, now, ma'am, we couldn't do that. Not when L.B. here is expecting.''

A brouhaha erupted around the table and escalated as the family attempted to digest this latest bomb. Victoria's mask fogged and her nostrils flared as she inhaled.

Elizabeth nudged Dakota. She didn't want to kill Victoria. Only to become disinherited. Quickly, she explained. ''No, no, we're not expecting just yet. We're, uh…well, we're expecting to expect a baby, and not really expecting now.''

The relief in the room was palpable.

Dakota's brows wiggled roguishly. ''But, it won't be long now, before L.B. has a bun in the oven. In fact, we probably won't be staying for dessert, if you catch my drift.''

''I'll say,'' Victoria roared. When she'd recovered sufficiently from her shock, she cast off her mask, pushed back her chair and stood. ''Elizabeth! You will join me in the study at once.'' The formidable spark in her eyes brooked no argument.

''Now?''

''Now.''

''But what about Dakota? I never go anywhere without him.''

''I'm sure he can spare you for a few minutes.''

Elizabeth looked properly pained at having to tear herself away from her ardent groom, even for a moment. ''Can you, honey? Really?''

Disgust tinged Charles's irreverent snort.

''Don't worry none about me, L.B. I'll just wait here with the family.'' Dakota was pleased to note that Rainbow blanched and clutched Ashby's hand. ''You run along. I'll be fine.''

Unable to resist the temptation, and feeling that it would

make a nice touch, Dakota stood and bent her back over the table for another outrageous kiss. When he broke the kiss and they righted themselves, he was breathing like a locomotive, and his heart was a roaring thunder in his ears.

It seemed the fun and games were beginning to get the better of him.

Chapter Five

Elizabeth rushed out of the dining room after Victoria. For someone who was knocking at death's door, the elderly woman was moving at a pretty good clip, oxygen tank and all.

"Grandmother, wait. I'd like to help you!"

"So you say," Victoria groused over her shoulder as she jerked her tank across the foyer floor. The heels of her impractical, yet fashionable, shoes clicked out her irritation in an angry Morse code.

Fantastic floor-to-ceiling double doors led to the east wing library and, giving the knob a vicious twist, Victoria shoved them open and barreled through, her tank careening to-and-fro behind her. "Elizabeth, come in here, and sit down." She flicked her fingers at a Louis the XIVth chair that was situated on a Turkish rug in front of her massive desk.

The library was paneled in a rich mahogany that glowed with a satiny sheen from the low, indirect lighting from both above and below the endless bookcases. A long ladder on a sliding track leaned against the far wall, and the floor-to-ceiling windows were draped in a rich cranberry damask. Tasteful busts of ancestors and other statuary were situated around the room on short, up-lighted granite display pillars. On the wall nearest Victoria's desk, a massive glass case held the many awards and trophies for excellence bestowed upon her company over the years.

Reluctantly, Elizabeth did as she was bid and took a seat in the heavily carved antique. Her gaze followed Victoria as the old girl flitted back and forth in front of the bay window behind her desk, too agitated to land in any one spot for more than an instant. The long, clear plastic tubing tangled beneath her feet as she paced.

Eyes narrow, tone clipped, Victoria spoke. "Would you care to explain to me what the devil is going on in there?"

Elizabeth, not certain what her grandmother did and did not know for sure, decided to play her cards close to her chest. "To what are you referring?"

"I'm referring to that clodhopping rube you call your husband, and the legion of children he intends to sire by you." She clapped her mask over her mouth and took a deep drag, then snatched it away and waved it about. "Please. Tell me this is another one of your tricks."

"Tricks?" She stared meaningfully at the oxygen mask.

"Don't get cheeky with me, girl. I want you to tell me that you are *not* serious when you say you are in love with this poster boy for the hoi polloi."

Elizabeth pushed at her cuticles with her thumbnail. "I *am* serious, Grandmother." That much at least, she was beginning to fear, was true. Not a particularly handy thing, developing feelings for Dakota, considering he'd told her on the way over here that he had no desire for any kind of permanent relationship. Nevertheless, her heart never had been much on logic, much to Victoria's eternal frustration. She lifted her eyes to meet her grandmother's gaze.

Victoria stopped pacing and looked at her for a solid, silent minute. Finally, "You are in love with him. I can see it in your eyes." Disgusted and weary beyond words, the elder woman pulled out the rolling chair from behind her desk and sagged into its buttery leather depths. The oxygen mask dangled from her fingertips. "Young lady, do you have any idea of the pitfalls of marrying outside your social class?"

"It's been done successfully before."

"Rarely."

"I can make it work. I've inherited pigheaded determination from my paternal grandmother."

"Touché." A grudging smile flirted with Victoria's lips, then submerged as she leaned forward and reverted to the formidable businesswoman who piloted an empire. Once again, her eyes grew steely and her lips, thin. "Elizabeth, you are young. Right now, you think you want the simple life while you have a sexy young stud in your bed. Of course, it all seems very beguiling from your immature vantage point."

Elizabeth dug her fingertips into the intricately carved handles of her chair. Jaw grim, she lifted a brow and stared back at the old crone who could so easily vacillate from Jekyll to Hyde, depending upon the amount of money at stake.

Gnarled fingers stabbed at the ink blotter. "But what about your future? What about when the time comes and you have a..." a spasm of revulsion crossed her face, "...brood of nine little brats and not enough money to feed and clothe them? You were not born and bred for such a dismal future. Your destiny is to run an empire, not give birth to one."

Elizabeth bit her tongue to keep from lashing back. How many times would they have this conversation? The names may have changed, but the tune was the same old funeral dirge. She was sick of being told what she was supposed to do with her life.

"Grandmother, I don't want to run an empire. Like my mother before me," Victoria's expression reflected pain at the mention of her daughter, but was quickly replaced by determination, "I want to live a simple life with a simple husband. I don't need jewelry and furs and fancy cars and servants to make me happy. I need love and warmth and a big mess and a lot of noise."

"At only twenty-seven years old, you're still just a child. You don't even know the meaning of happiness!"

Elizabeth gasped, flabbergasted at how out of touch Victoria could be with anything that resembled an emotion. "And *you* do?"

"I know that happiness is fleeting state of mind that can come and go. But a family fortune will sustain you through the bad times." A calculating look flashed into Victoria's eyes. "I've worked too hard to build this company into what my own grandmother dreamed it could mean to the women in our family. And I'll be damned if I'm going to let another woman in this family throw her own future away over some ridiculous dream of being poor!"

"Grandmother, the thing you fail to realize is, it's *my* future."

Victoria pressed her fingertips to her temples and closed her eyes. Her thick, dark lashes were a stark contrast to a complexion drained of color. The artificial red of her cheeks and lips seemed suddenly too bright. After a long, uncomfortable silence, Victoria exhaled in defeat. When she finally spoke, her voice held a genuine hint of nostalgia.

"Life," she began so softly that Elizabeth did a double take, "isn't all about love, you know. I discovered that myself when I was a young girl." She lifted her lashes and, though her gaze was trained on her granddaughter, Elizabeth knew she wasn't seeing her. Instead, Victoria was gazing into her past. "I too, had a chance to marry a man of meager means. For love."

"You did?" Brow wrinkled, jaw slack, Elizabeth stared at her grandmother. Victoria in love? Though she tried to picture it in her mind's eye, the image was elusive. Even so, she had the funniest feeling that for once, Victoria was being square with her.

"Yes. In fact your…Dakota, there, reminds me a little of my Matthew."

"Your…Matthew? He *does?*" Would wonders never cease?

"Yes. Matt was a wonderful young man. Full of the dickens." A gentle smile played at her lips. "My first love. And, my last. Even though I married your grandfather Luther and had two children with him, I don't think I ever got over Matt."

"What happened?"

"When I was a young college age girl, we saw each other in secret over one blissful summer when I was home from school. He was the son of a groomsman for one of our polo pony stables. Had a real way with horses, and something about his roguish, reckless nature reminds me of your Dakota. We fell in love. And just before I was to return to school, he asked me to marry him."

"And you said no? Why?"

"Because," Victoria's eyes fluttered open, "my parents would have had a fit, that's why! I chose the company instead of love. I owed it to my mother. To my grandmother. To my family. To…*you.* And someday, your children. I had enough sense to know that once the thrill wore off with him, I'd be bored. And worse, disowned by my family. And then what? I'd be the penniless wife of a groomsman's son.'' She took a deep breath and let it out, mindless of the oxygen mask now. ''Oh, I will admit, I was sorely tempted to follow my heart. But I could see in doing so, it would eventually lead to disaster. The way it did for your own mother.''

Elizabeth let her head fall back against her shoulders and shot a rueful smile at the ceiling. ''You knew that, huh?''

''Yes. And I don't regret my decision.''

''You don't?'' Elizabeth couldn't believe that anyone could find emotional solace in cold, hard cash. ''Honestly?'' she probed, ''you have no regrets?''

Victoria went deaf, when it suited her purpose. ''We lead a privileged life, Elizabeth.''

''It's not my privilege.''

''We will see about that. In fact—'' Victoria seemed to suddenly remember that she was courting the Grim Reaper and began to hack and wheeze in a most impressive manner. She grappled with her oxygen mask, got it turned right side up and took several dramatic breaths. After her recovery was sufficient, she continued feebly. ''—I'm going to have to ask you a favor, and being that you are here, I don't see that there is any reason you can't help. It's the least you can do, all things considered.'' She peeped at Elizabeth from behind the foggy plastic cup that covered her mouth and nose.

Elizabeth sighed. ''What do you need?''

More respiratory distress pitched Victoria about. She held up a hand to buy some time. Her lashes fluttered in a most theatrical manner until she could gasp, ''As you can see, I'm far too ill to venture out. I need you to stand in for me at a Lindon House preview down at the Autumn

Leaf tomorrow night.'' Before Elizabeth could protest, Victoria continued, sounding weaker by the moment. ''It won't take you long. I'm introducing a new line of men's products, some skin care, aftershave, soaps, that sort of thing. You need only make some brief remarks and do a few product demonstrations. I will send detailed instructions with you, as well as a prewritten speech.'' Victoria pushed the intercom button on her desk. ''Margaret, bring the gurney, I'm feeling ill.''

''Yes ma'am,'' came the tinny reply.

''Tomorrow night?'' The little hairs at the back of Elizabeth's neck that worked as radar when Victoria was up to something, stood at attention and she couldn't keep the note of accusation out of her voice. ''I don't suppose Bernard will be there?''

Another attack of coughing left Victoria winded and she slumped in her chair. ''He was invited, yes. Monaco's *is* our biggest customer after all and this will be an extremely important show for all of our clients.''

''How convenient. Grandmother, even if it weren't for Dakota, I would never marry Bernard.''

This feebly, ''But he loves you.''

''He loves building his little empire. I can't believe I'm still discussing Bernard with you, let alone allowing you to talk me into being in the same room with him tomorrow night. I shouldn't even go to this thing,'' she muttered under her breath.

''Elizabeth, you wouldn't deny a dying woman.''

She swallowed a scream. ''Of course not. You can count on me. But, just so you'll know, I'm bringing Dakota.''

Again, Victoria stabbed at the intercom button. ''Margaret, my heart medication.'' She averted her gaze to the window and stared out for a long moment, seeming to attempt to come to terms with the fact that she could exhibit only so much control over her granddaughter. "If it is the only way that I can get you to attend, then…so be it."

Upon returning to her suite, Elizabeth found Dakota already lounging in her parlor area, his stocking feet propped on the arm of the sofa in which he lay. He'd changed out of Charles's suit and into a pair of blue jeans and a snug white T-shirt. The television in the entertainment center was tuned to the sports channel and the delectable aroma of pepperoni pizza wafted to greet her from an open box on the coffee table. She had the absurd urge to shout a cheerful, "Hi, honey, I'm home!"

The domestic scene in front of her was a childhood fantasy of normalcy come true. She swallowed against the lump of joy that burned in her throat.

"*No,* you stupid *jerk!* Open your eyes! *Awwww* man!" Growling and hollering as if the referee might benefit from his wisdom, Dakota hauled himself to a sitting position and brandished his remote control at the football game on the screen. "For pity's sake, are you *blind?* That was not a *fumble!* Any imbecile could see that!"

Elizabeth shut the door behind her and kicked off the cowboy boots that Dakota had brought for her. "Hi."

Head jerking around so that he could see back over his shoulder, Dakota sent her a lopsided grin, then turned his focus back to the game. "Hey, babe. Just a second and I'll be…right…*No!*" he screamed, his complexion flushing ruddy as he shook his fists at the set. "No, you stupid, stupid fool! *Auuggghhh.* Look! Look! There, see? I'm right! You can see it perfectly on the replay!" He fell back against the couch and groaned, then rallied and shot another glance back at her. "I took the liberty of ordering pizza delivery, L.B., since you never made it back to the table. Figured you'd be hungry after going a few rounds with old Vicky." He patted the cushion at his side. "Join me."

Elizabeth wanted to cry. The extreme bliss of this moment was almost more than she could bear.

"Beer? I brought some in my prop bag." Dakota held up a frosty cold one from the six-pack on the coffee table. "Goes great with football."

"Love one. Thanks. You are a pleasure to come home to, husband."

He grinned as she joined him on the couch. After prying the top off the bottle with an opener, he held it out and their fingers brushed during the handoff, sending warm tingles of happiness straight to the core of her being. The sweating bottle dripped on her dress and the cold liquid burned a trail down her throat. She pulled a heavy, stringy slice of pizza onto a paper plate and took a healthy bite. How had he known she'd be famished? Never had she met anyone so thoughtful. She made a mental note to reimburse him for the food.

"So, talk to me, sweetheart." A soft drink jingle filled the airwaves. "Commercial." He aimed the remote at the TV and the catchy ditty grew dim. "I was beginning to wonder if you were going to make it out of there alive."

Elizabeth nodded, her mouth full. "Me, too." She swallowed. "Sorry that took so long, but Victoria had a curve ball or two to lob in my direction, as usual." She licked her fingers and then took another swig of beer. This was so wonderful. She noticed that he'd already dispensed with several slices of pizza himself.

"Didn't you get enough to eat at dinner tonight?"

Dakota tore his eyes away from the stats that flashed on the screen. "No, not really." He chuckled. "I don't think anyone ate too much tonight. Everyone was still a little shell-shocked at having Junior Sample from *Hee Haw* join their ranks.''

''How did it go, after I left?''

''I think you'd have been proud. There's a big old wine stain in the middle of the tablecloth now, but I told Charles not to worry about it, the centerpiece covers most of it just fine.'' Eyes twinkling with dry humor, he pushed his bottle between his lips and took a pull.

Her grin was so deep, it tickled her stomach. ''How'd that happen?''

''Oh, I got to demonstrating a few roping techniques with an extension cord, and missed.''

Elizabeth slumped against her arm of the couch and let the laughter flow. ''Oh, I wish I could have seen that. Shoot.''

''You didn't miss all that much. After the ropin' demo, I mostly explained about our life together. You and I are avid gamblers, by the way, when we are not bowling or camping and hunting. Thought Rainbow would expire right there on the spot when I explained how we like to go out on the weekends and lob grenades at Bambi and Thumper and the gang.'' He gave his chest a lazy scratching. ''Oh, and everyone was horrified by our square dancing lessons. Seems they don't appreciate my calling abilities. I was just a little too far out in allemande-left field for their taste, I'm afraid.''

''Ohhhh.'' Elizabeth let her pizza drop to the paper plate on the coffee table and clutched her stomach. Her eyes squeezed shut, and she laughed until it hurt.

''I licked my plate clean, stacked my dishes, then stacked everyone else's—a little prematurely, if the miffed looks on their faces were anything to go by, but hell, they eat so damn slow. Anyhow, I brought 'em to the kitchen, came back out with the coffeepot and freshened their cups.

I left a tip under my dessert plate for the guy who brings the plates back and forth from the kitchen.''

"Stop!" she begged and gasped for air. "You're killing me." On the cushion next to him her feet flailed and she threw a decorative pillow at his head.

Dimples in full bloom, Dakota grabbed her stocking feet, pulled them into his lap and began to rub her toes. It was heavenly. "So, how'd the meeting with Nanna go?"

Tears still streamed down her cheeks, and sniffing, she swiped at them. "Oh, not nearly as much fun as dinner, I'm sure. As usual, our conversation was fraught with frustration and condemnation." She wiggled her toes. "Mmm. Thank you, that feels wonderful. If you are interested in the job, I'd be willing to hire you for this purpose after all my shifts at Ned's." She heaved an audible exhalation of ecstasy.

"I could probably be persuaded." Dakota chuckled and moved his deft ministrations to the arch of her foot. "So, what all did Victoria have to say?"

"Well, she asked me to stand in for her tomorrow night as hostess of her Lindon House preview. Twice a year she puts on a chichi business soiree for the local jet set, down at the Autumn Leaf Hotel. It's for the buyers and the press and…well for anyone who is anyone, if you get my drift. They are a real drag. Anyway, she claims she's too sick to make an appearance, but I know better. You saw how she bolted out of the dining room."

"Yeah, she was movin' fast enough to compete in a barrel ridin' event without the horse, I'll tell you that right now."

He pushed his thumbs into her heel and moved them in slow, gentle circles. "The Autumn Leaf Hotel, huh?"

She swallowed a moan of pleasure. "Um-hmm."

"Them's swanky digs."

"You've been?"

He cleared his throat. "Heard."

"Ah. Well, now you are going to get the chance to see, firsthand because I caved in and promised her that I'd pinch-hit. You're coming with me by the way. Told her I needed an assistant to help me demonstrate the products. Sorry about that."

"Demonstrate?" He pulled a funny face. "You did say this is a makeup company?"

Elizabeth giggled. "Yes, but don't worry. This time the products are for men. Aftershave, lotions, that kind of junk."

He looked only slightly mollified. "I can do that, I guess."

"I think you can, too. In fact," she lifted her head off the arm of the couch and sent him a meaningful look, "I think that we might be able to further our efforts to become disinherited. Victoria likes to say her parties are *nulli se- cundus* in the makeup world."

Dakota snorted. "Yeah, well, it might be second to none now, but it's gonna be third string when we get done with it, trust me."

Brows drawn together in thought, Elizabeth peeked at him from beneath her heavy lids and wondered how he knew Latin. From the sound of things, all that money spent on her going to private school had been wasted. Dakota was a constant source of amazement and delight.

"Bernard is going to be there, by the way."

Dakota's forehead wrinkled. "Oh?"

"Yes. He's a major player in our business. His family's business gave Lindon House its start."

"Ah. I'm beginning to get the picture. You know," he continued, switching his attention to her other foot, "it's pretty obvious that Victoria is faking her illness."

"Yes?" Elizabeth nodded, wondering where he was going with this.

"I just can't help but wonder if she has something up her sleeve."

"Wouldn't be the first time. What do you think she's up to?"

"I think she is hoping that by standing in for her tomorrow, you will get a taste for everything she finds so compelling about the world of high finance. It can be very compelling, you know."

The faint roar of the crowd from the TV set drew his attention for a moment, and he clutched her foot. "For crying out loud," he muttered under his breath, then, with a shake of his head, turned his attention back to her.

Again, Elizabeth stared at him. "How do you know about the allure of the world of high finance?"

He shrugged as a sheepish grin tugged at his beautiful, sculpted lips. "Heard. Anyhow, Victoria probably thinks that you'll be so enchanted with Bernard's polished manners and that I'll be such a hayseed by comparison, that you will eventually see the light and be only too eager to have our marriage annulled."

"Never." Elizabeth laughed out loud. "I promised to stick by you for better or worse, until the end of this weekend, and I meant it."

"That's my girl."

Dakota's sexy, lazily hooded gaze suddenly had her heartbeat roaring in her ears. Luckily, his team made another grievous mistake, and he was forced to throw her feet off his lap and leap from the couch to threaten physical harm to the TV.

Sometime later, after a relaxing evening of televised sports, pizza and lengthy, wonderful conversation spent getting to know one another a little better, it was—much to Dakota's dismay—time to call it a night.

As valiant as her effort was to stay awake, Elizabeth was yawning. No small wonder. After pulling a full shift at Ned's then coming here to verbally spar with her exhausting family, it was amazing she was still awake at all. From the hallway, the gentle tones of a grandfather clock chimed the late hour.

"Eleven already? Where did the evening go?" Again, Elizabeth yawned broadly and stretched.

Dakota's head wagged from side to side. Scooting to the edge of the sofa, he began to tidy up the coffee table. When she tried to help, he pushed her hands away. "You look beat. Why don't I take care of this mess and you go settle down for the night?"

Slow and sleepy, a smile tugged at her features. "You really are the most wonderful husband, dear. I'm sorry if our nine kids and I don't tell you that more often." In a teasing manner, she leaned against him, punch-drunk with weariness and giggled.

Chin tucked into his shoulder, he looked down at her with a grin. "Oh, now Little Bit, you know I live to serve you and our tykes." More than anything, he wanted to pull her into his arms and kiss her, this time, without an audience. But it wouldn't be right. Not at this stage of the game anyway. If he was going to woo her, to change her mind about marriage, to help her forget the trauma done by the possibility of an arranged marriage to old Bernard, then he was going to have to move slowly. So, instead, he gave her a casual pat on the back, then took a deep breath and held it for several beats. "You get. Don't worry about me. I can find my own bed."

She stretched, arms high, face scrunched, back arched

and let out a weary groan. "Deal. See you in the morning." She paused on her way to her room. "And Dakota?"

"Yeah?"

"Thanks. For everything." Growing a bit flustered, she touched her tongue to her lips. "You were very...convincing tonight. I know that you probably have lots of other opportunities for social engagements this weekend with other, you know, friends, but I promise, I'll make this whole thing worth your while."

"Don't worry about it. To be honest, this is the most fun I've had in a long time."

Her face lit with pleasure. "Me, too." After they'd stared at each other for a moment, the pause grew slightly awkward. She waved a hand behind her, gesturing to her room and its adjoining bath. "Well, I should probably do as you say and get. Night."

"Night."

He watched the gentle sway of her shapely derriere as she sauntered out of the room and into her master bath, closing the large double doors behind her. He stood for a moment just absorbing the cozy ambiance. So this is what it would be like to be married to Elizabeth. Even his most creative daydreams couldn't beat the fantastic reality.

The sounds of running water and her soft hum serenaded him as he stuffed empty beer bottles and the pizza container in a wastebasket. With the stack of unused napkins, he polished the tabletop and pitched them. Then, he tossed the decorative pillows back onto the sofa, turned off the TV and the lamps and headed to his bathroom to brush his teeth.

He'd no sooner stripped down to his boxers and slipped between the sheets when there came a knock at the door to the suite. Bolting upright in bed, his wild gaze darted about. Okay. Stay calm. Someone was wanting to come into Elizabeth's suite. Someone who could see that he was sleeping in the wrong bed. He swung his legs out from under the covers, and hit the floor running. Time to make the bed. Fast. Hurriedly, he flung the blankets up into place, tucked them in the best he could, smashed the pillow into shape and kicked his clothes under the dust ruffle and beneath the bed.

"Elizabeth!" he hissed. From the sound of things, she was still in the master bath, preparing for bed. *"Elizabeth!"* Dragging his duffel bag behind him, he stumbled through the darkness toward her room.

Another knock sounded at the door, this time louder. More impatient.

"Elizabeth!"

"Accckkk!" Startled, as she came out of the bathroom and into her room, she let out a shriek and they collided. Dakota dropped the handle to his duffel bag and supporting her around the waist with his arm, steadied her before she could slip to the floor. She was wearing a modest nylon nightie, but it was so soft and thin, he could feel the curve of her hip beneath his fingertips.

"Shhhh!" He clapped the palm of his free hand over her mouth.

She struggled against him, her hands pushing against the pectoral muscles of his bare chest. *"Whaaa?!"*

"Quiet! Someone's at the door." Her hands stilled and he wondered if she could feel how hard he was breathing at the moment. "I just made my bed—sort of—and thought I should come in here with you, being that we're married and all." When she nodded in understanding, he peeled his hand away from her lips.

Another thundering knock at the door.

She cleared her throat. "Who is it?" she called, sweetly.

"It's me. Victoria. I need to see you for a moment,"

came the feeble reply. The sounds of muffled coughing filtered to them from the hallway.

"Just a minute!" she sang at the door. To Dakota she whispered, *"Come on."*

The faint glow of her bedside lamp lit the way as she grabbed his hand, and pulled him into her bedroom. They rushed to the bed, dived under the covers and thrashed about for a moment to make it look as if some sort of nocturnal connubial recreation had taken place. Dakota flung all of her embroidered, decorative pillows off the bed like so many lacy missiles, and the few stuffed dolls that had been propped on those, followed. Face flushed, and hair staticky, Elizabeth sat up and surveyed their handiwork.

"Good. Looks just about right, don't you think?"

He yanked the bedspread off the bed and tossed it in a heap at the side of the bed. Then, propped on his elbow, he smiled a lazy smile at her, thinking that it did indeed look just about right. "Only thing I can think that would add to the ambiance would be a burning cigarette."

Elizabeth giggled. "I don't smoke."

He grinned. "Then I guess we're ready."

She leapt out of the bed and rushed to the door. Upon opening it, Victoria barreled in, huffing on her oxygen mask. The tank was in the hallway, and the tubing had come unhooked but the older woman didn't seem to notice.

"Grandmother! What a surprise! What can I do for you at this hour?"

"What do you mean, this hour?" she crabbed. She gathered her shawl about her shoulders, which Elizabeth thought, was a nice touch. "What are you talking about? It's early! Maybe out on the farm you bed down with the chickens, but here in the big city, where we civilized people live, business is routinely conducted in the evening."

She shot a suspicious glance beyond the parlor and into Elizabeth's bedroom. Dakota waved to her through the pillared archway where he lay in bed, and grinned a cocky grin. "Hey, Nanna! What's up?"

A feral growl, so low Elizabeth could barely hear it rumbled in her grandmother's throat and she inhaled deeply from her useless mask. Elizabeth's eyes traced the path of her grandmother's narrowed gaze. Her own breathing quickened and became shallow, but for completely different reasons than Victoria's.

The sight was not one a person could easily forget. Have mercy. Victoria wasn't the only one who needed oxygen.

Dakota's naked torso, all sinewy and muscular glowed a lovely shade of tan under the soft light of her bedside lamp. His bicep muscles bulged, as he lay upon her bed, his silky brown head propped in one hand, elbow to pillow and the other arm resting across his flat abdomen. One foot dangled out from beneath the sheets that clung to his lower body, outlining long, powerful legs and a most adorable behind. The feel of his steely chest—as she'd clung to him in the doorway, only moments ago—came flooding back, and her cheeks grew warm.

The playful invitation in his eyes was unmistakable as he looked at her, those rakish dimples bracketing the sides of his mouth.

"I, uh…" she tore her gaze from her bed and forced herself to focus on Victoria. "…what did you need, Grandmother?"

Victoria thrust an overflowing file folder into her arms. "Here," her words were punctuated by sharp coughs, "are my notes for tomorrow night. If you start reading right now, you might be ready by the time it starts." She darted a pointed glare at Dakota.

Elizabeth stared at her hands and stammered. "Bu…

but…but you said that I wouldn't have to do that much—''

Her grandmother cut her off. ''Elizabeth, you'll need to know some of this product information, or you will come off looking like a fool. It won't hurt you to acquaint yourself with the product analysis reports, the market comparisons, stock potential, chemical composition, test market results, pending advertising campaigns, testimonials, Lindon House financial reports,'' she patted the folder with an age-spotted hand, ''it's all in there.''

Elizabeth turned a dull glance to Dakota, then back to Victoria. ''Sounds fascinating.''

With a curt nod, Victoria tottered through the parlor and into the hallway. ''If you have questions, I'll be up. For the past couple months, I've suffered dreadfully from insomnia.''

Elizabeth rolled her eyes.

''Don't let the bedbugs bite,'' Dakota hollered.

Victoria harrumphed and was gone.

Exhaling long and slow, Elizabeth closed her door and padded from the parlor into her bedroom. She climbed onto the foot of the bed and lobbed the file to the center of the mattress where it landed with a thud. ''This,'' she said dismally and waved a dismissive hand, ''is precisely why I don't want the job. I hate this kind of stuff. Market analysis. Blech.'' She stuck out her tongue, and Dakota laughed.

''Oh, now, it's not that bad.''

Elizabeth moaned and flopped face first crosswise on the bed, where she lay juxtaposed with him. ''How do you know?'' she mumbled into the rumpled sheets.

He grinned. In her own way, she was as dramatic as old Vicky. ''Heard.''

She lifted her head and stared at him through bleary eyes. "You sure do hear about a lot of stuff."

"Good listener."

Her laughter was a low, husky rumble that had Dakota's pulse ticking up tempo. In a mirrored pose, she propped herself up on her elbow and regarded him with midnight eyes. "Yes, you are."

"Aw, shucks."

To keep from going all dopey-eyed and staring, he dragged the file toward him and opening it, began to shuffle through the various pages. Just as Victoria had said, it was all in there. With a jaded eye, he scanned the columns, flow charts and profit indexes, and though this was a simple cursory glance, he was impressed. Victoria ran a tight ship. It wouldn't hurt Elizabeth to know some of this information. In his humble opinion, Victoria was right. Family members should know what's going on with the business.

He glanced up at her. "What say we go over some of this stuff? I can give you a hand."

"Let's not..." she yawned a wide, squeaky yawn and let her head slide from her palm, down her arm and to the crook of her elbow, "and say we did. I think ignorance is bliss."

"Nah. Knowledge is power."

"Mmm." Her eyes drifted shut. "Okay then, read aloud. I can sleep learn."

Again, an intrusive knock thundered at her door.

"Aaahhh!" Elizabeth rolled onto her stomach and wailed on the mattress with her fists. "Who is it?"

"It's me. Victoria."

Elizabeth mumbled, "Come to spy on us, no doubt and make sure we're doing our homework."

"Come on in, Nanna," Dakota shouted. "Door's open."

"*Dakota!*" Scrambling, Elizabeth crawled from the foot of the bed and dived under the covers next to him.

"Mmm. Now this is more like it," he purred. Eyes flashing with mischief, he pulled Elizabeth—sputtering all the while—over to his side and tucked her head onto his chest. With lazy fingers, he began to stroke her hair.

"Hey, look who's here, sugar lips. It's Nanna, come to visit us again. Hey, Nanna."

Victoria, as was becoming her habit, ignored him and spoke to Elizabeth. "I forgot to include the prewritten speeches that you are to deliver tomorrow night."

"Don't worry, Nanna," Dakota piped up, "you're not interrupting anything. Yet." He wiggled his brows in a rakish manner. "But, if we're ever going to get around to giving you that great-grandbaby to bounce on your knee, you're going to have to give us some time alone. If—" he paused for effect "—you know what I mean."

"I was most certainly not worried about interrupting." Gaze chilly, Victoria tossed the speeches onto Elizabeth's nightstand.

"Good, good. 'Cause, you're welcome almost any old time."

Without a word, Victoria spun around and marched out of the suite, crashing the door shut behind her.

They lay frozen for a moment, listening as Victoria's footsteps grew faint. Silence fell.

"Hear that?" Dakota asked.

"No, what?"

"It's the sound of Victoria crossin' you out of her will as we speak."

"Dare we dream?" Elizabeth groaned and rolled off Dakota's chest and onto a pillow. "Nice job with the baby thing. That really gets her support hose in a twist."

Head thrown back, her silky hair fanned out over the

crisp linens and her face, angelic in the ethereal light of the lamp, Elizabeth Derovencourt had never looked more beautiful to him. So smooth and soft was her complexion, so perfect and straight were her teeth, so plump and kiss-able her dewy lips, she reminded him of an old-time movie starlet, posing for a pinup. Her heavy fringe of lashes, nat-urally dark, hooded sparkling eyes as she gazed up at him.

"What do you want to bet she'll be back?"

Tone droll, Dakota said, "I wouldn't put it past her." He sat up, needing to put some distance between himself and this woman who fascinated him more with each pass-ing second. "Anyway, I should let you get some sleep. Sounds like we have a big day ahead of us tomorrow."

"An endlessly boring one at any rate."

"Oh, I don't know about that." He gathered the speeches and file folder into a stack and held it up for her to see. "Mind if I take a peek?"

"If that stuff turns you on, be my guest."

It didn't turn him on nearly as much as the beauty who lay in the bed next to him, but that was a moot point. "Thanks." A swift peck on her cheek, and he was out of her bed and in the armchair at the other side of the room. Where it was safe.

He smiled and winked. "I'll just sit here and read until the coast is clear."

Elizabeth's eyelids slid shut and she smiled. "Mm-kay. I'll just lie here and rest my eyes."

Within moments, her breathing was slow and steady. Dakota lifted his gaze from the documents in his hand, and watched her sleep with a yearning he'd never known be-fore.

Chapter Six

The strains of Dakota's shower the next morning slowly brought Elizabeth out of a delicious dream, where she'd been making macaroni and cheese for her nine happy, barefoot, streaked-with-dirt-from-playing-in-the-backyard, kids. Much to her patriotic father-in-law's delight, all of her dimpled offspring were named for past presidents of these United States. There was George, Abraham, Ulysses, Franklin, Grover, Woodrow, Calvin, Herbert and little Teddy. And, her husband—who looked suspiciously like Dakota—shouted at a small black-and-white TV from the living room of their mobile home.

It was bliss.

And the best part? Victoria was happy for her and had even taken up knitting, when she wasn't reading to, or playing with her brood of great-grandchildren.

Elizabeth stretched languorously and then kicked her covers back. Pushing herself to a seated position, she raked her hands through her hair and glanced around her sterile, neat-as-a-pin room. The only concession to any kind of homey chaos was the pile of lacy pillows that Dakota had flung hither and yon, Victoria's file folder lying askew on the ottoman to the armchair and an afghan puddled on the floor nearby. Sometime after midnight, she'd roused for a moment and seen him still there sitting in the shadowed glow of a solitary lamp, thoughtfully scratching his shadowed jaw and pondering one of these myriad documents. Strange, a cowboy like him being so interested in those boring reports on men's skin care products. He didn't seem the type. They had to be dry as day-old toast.

There were still so many facets of his wonderful personality she had yet to discover.

She could her him humming in his shower and reached for her bedside phone to call the kitchen line. Breakfast for two would arrive shortly before she'd completed her own shower. Occasionally, she had to concede, there were certain advantages to being rich.

Dakota was reading the paper over coffee when she emerged from her bathroom, dressed in a breezy floral sundress and ready to take on the day.

"How did you sleep?" she asked, rounding the sofa. As she settled in next to him, she focused on a point beyond his ruggedly handsome face and tried to affect a casual attitude that said she wasn't as impressed with the way he filled out his black western shirt and faded jeans as she actually was.

"Like a log. I accidentally dozed off in that chair in your room. Sorry about that."

"Don't be. I kept thinking Grandmother would come back again to check on us. You never know. Plus, on the bright side, we don't have to make your bed to impress the maids."

"True." He arched that rakish brow that always had the

tips of her ears burning hot. Swallowing hard, she struggled for composure and inclined her head.

"Whatcha reading?"

"Financial section."

"Yeah?" Once again, she tried not to reveal her surprise. She'd taken him for a sports page kind of guy.

"Yeah. Nanna's shindig is in here." He held the paper up so she could see the headline and accompanying photo of Lindon House's latest offerings. "Sounds like it's gonna be a pretty big deal."

"Mmm. They always are." She poured herself a cup of coffee and bringing it to her lips, blew across the rim. "We should probably do some brainstorming about how to best handle this function. You know, how to act, what to wear, that kind of thing."

"I'm leaning toward the chaps."

Elizabeth laughed and took a sip. "For me or for you?"

"Only brought one pair. But, I'd be happy to share." His grin was infectious. "This thing could be a lot of fun, you know."

She lowered her voice in a conspiratorial manner. "I was thinking we should probably get out of here. The walls have ears, if you get my drift."

"Your wish is my command. I'm yours for the weekend, remember?"

Goose bumps shivered up her spine even as she cradled the steaming hot cup in her hands. How could she forget? "You swim?"

"Yep."

"Fish?"

"There are fish in your pool?"

Elizabeth laughed. "No, in the lake silly."

"What lake?"

"The one in the backyard. It's stocked with catfish. Victoria's got a dock with a little changing house where she keeps spare swimsuits and towels and stuff. We can go fishing or take the boat to the island.''

"Island?'' Dakota scratched his head. "Just how big is her yard?''

"It's a *small* island.'' Teasing him, she held up a limp wrist and affected a breezy pose. "Modest. Tasteful. You'll like it. I do. It's the one place where Victoria isn't inclined to follow and harangue me about taking over her business.''

He dropped the paper. "What are we waiting for?''

"I'll call the kitchen and have them make us some lunch food that goes good with barbecue catfish.''

"Sounds great. While you do that, I'll just run into my room and call the ranch. See how things are going.''

"Dakota? That you?''

Dakota tucked the phone between his shoulder and his ear and leaned back on his bed. "Yeah, Fuzzy, it's me. Is that bonehead brother of mine hangin' around?''

"Aayap. Around here somewhere.'' Fuzzy noisily sucked something from between his teeth. "Say, he told us that you're up there in Dallas pretendin' to be married to some lipstick tycoon's granddaughter.''

Dakota rolled his eyes. "He's got a big mouth.''

"So?''

"So, what?''

"So, howz it goin'? Me and the boys have a pool about whether or not this is gonna work. Hear tell she thinks you're dirt poor, and that's why she's taken a shine to ya. Montana says she's payin' ya and everything.''

"Yep.''

Raspy cackling rumbled over the line. "That's a hoot.''

In the background, Dakota could hear Red flipping him some guff about something.

"Hey, boss," Fuzzy chortled, "Red wants to know if you can bring some of them fancy skin care samples home. He's got a wart on his—"

"Yeah, yeah, you guys are a laugh a minute. Just tell Montana I called to check up on you idiots. He's got my cell phone number if there's a problem."

"Sure bet, boss." More hilarity in the background. "Boss, Red says he's got that not-so-fresh feeling. Can you bring him sumthin' for that?" Roaring laughter echoed throughout the stable's offices.

Dakota rolled his eyes and dropped the phone into its cradle. He was never going to live this down.

"I'm sorry that you had to hear all that." Elizabeth's muffled voice reached Dakota from her dressing stall in the breezy white poolhouse that served both the Olympic-size pool and the small lake on the property behind the mansion. They were in the process of changing into swimsuits that Victoria kept out there for guests.

"No problem." Without asking, he knew Elizabeth was referring to a shouting match so loud that—though it originated in the dining room—it had assaulted them upon exiting her third-floor suite. As they'd descended the stairs to pick up the lunch she'd ordered from the kitchen, the heated voices escalated, casting aspersions, hurling recriminations, and assassinating characters. And those were the pleasantries.

Dakota's outlandish behavior from the night before had been the primary target for most of the waspish comments, although Elizabeth had not escaped entirely unscathed. For himself, Dakota didn't care. But when they began to attack Elizabeth's decision to lead her own life in her own way, he had been tempted to storm in there and give them something worth talking about. However, for her sake, he'd kept his cool.

Elizabeth sighed. "It *is* a problem. A big one. I can't apologize enough. No matter how often I hear them bicker and fight, I never really seem to get used to how vicious they can be."

"Don't be sorry. It's not your fault." In the stall next door to hers, Dakota unbuckled his belt and tugging his T-shirt from the waistband of his jeans, stripped it off over his head and draped it over a hook. "To be honest, I thought the stuff they said about me was kind of funny. Especially the part Rainbow said about my being a—how did she phrase that again?"

"Oh. Uh, I believe she called you a bovine murdering carnivore." An indignant sound issued from deep in her throat. "Anyway, just because you work as a cattle ranch foreman is no reason to talk about you in such derogatory terms."

Dakota laughed. "Yes, but isn't that the whole point? To get them to hate me?"

Elizabeth sighed. "Yes, but even so, I'm mortified. What if we really were married?"

He could fairly hear the hackles rising and he was touched by her fierce defense of his character. "Hey, L.B.," his pet name had become a teasing endearment, "don't fret. I promise I'll get over it."

"Oh, I know, but that's still no excuse for their cruelty. Listen Dakota—"

The sounds of a zipper coming down and pumps being flung off her feet and bouncing off the wall reminded him that soon he'd get to see her in that little black number that she'd tugged from a drawer. The very thought, had his pulses singing and his hands fumbling with the buttons to his fly. He eased his faded jeans down over his hips and hung them by a belt loop next to his T-shirt.

"Yeah?" He picked up the navy swim trunks he'd chosen and shook them out.

"I, well, I just want you to know that *I* don't think that you would be an awful choice for a husband at all."

Dakota froze, balancing on one foot, midgrapple for the leg hole of his trunks with the other foot.

"In fact I would be proud to be…uh, ouch," the sounds of her spandex snapping into place reached him, "you know, be your wife."

Stunned and elated by her words, he fell back against the wall and struggled to remain upright. She would be proud to be his *wife?* The victory roar of the crowd from last night's football game swelled in his head. He cleared his throat and emitted a strangled, "Oh?"

She paused for an uncomfortable beat, then her words tumbled out in a hurry. "Sure. If circumstances were different, of course."

The disappointed *"Ohhhh,"* of the crowd replaced their previously jubilant cheer.

"I know that you were commandeered into this mess, and not really looking for a bunch of in-law hassles as a way to spend your weekend and—"

"I—" he groped for the perfect words to tell her how much this special time together meant to him, without frightening her off, but Elizabeth rushed on, seeming nearly afraid of the silence.

"And I want you to know that I respect that. I know what it's like to be shoved into a relationship that you didn't really want, and I'm just so grateful that you were willing to help me out anyway. I've really got to hand it to you. You've been a wonderful sport."

A wonderful sport. "Oh. Right."

He slid down the wall to the bench in the stall where he landed with a thud. *She would be proud to be his wife? Under different circumstances?* What did that mean? What circumstances? And what did she mean when she talked about being shoved into a relationship she didn't want? Is that how she felt about Bernard? Or…him? In that moment, myriad thoughts flashed through his mind, leaving him feeling at once hopeful and defeated.

Her nervous laughter filled the silence and made him wonder if she was simply trying to assuage his feelings for her family's behavior toward him.

Eyes closed, he reminded himself for the umpteenth time that she was tired of constraints and wanted a life of freedom. Marriage held no appeal for her. And could he blame her? Hers was a pathetic role model for a loving family. No wonder she wanted no part of that trap.

But could he make her see that it could be different?

Even though he'd spent pretty much every weekday of the last two months in her company at Ned's, it was still early in the relationship, he reminded himself. Just because he'd long ago fallen head over heels, didn't mean she felt the same. Yet. But hopefully, he could change her mind. And soon.

For, the more time he spent in Elizabeth Derovencourt's company, the more he came to need her. To want her.

The *snick* of her bolt lock sliding back and her door opening had him coming back to the present and fumbling with the drawstring at his waist. From the sound of things, she was dressed and ready to go.

"Elizabeth—"

"Hmm?"

He threw open his own lock and stepped out of his dressing room. And stopped cold.

There she stood, looking for all the world like some

mythical Greek goddess, preparing to smooth sunscreen onto her shapely calves. A shimmering patch of sun from the skylight bathed her, setting her lithe body on fire and causing her hair to shine like burnished gold.

"Damn." The hoarse word unconsciously slipped past his lips and he swallowed hard. As he gazed at her, his lungs constricted and his heartbeat kicked up a notch. She was perfect. Exquisite.

The suit was cut high on the thigh and dipped low in the front accentuating the length of her spectacular legs and the lush fullness of her bust. Her creamy skin glowed tan against the shiny black fabric, and he marveled at how sleek she looked. He fought the sudden urge to step the two or three strides it would take to reach her and pull her into his arms and press her incredible body against his own and kiss her until she was just as breathless as he was now.

She paused in her task and shot him an inquiring glance. "Something wrong?"

"Ah…" he gave his head a clearing shake. He'd been going to say something, but he couldn't for the life of him remember what. He improvised. "Uh, no I just was, thinking, uh, damn, I forgot to pack my suntan lotion." He frowned and silently berated himself. That was inane.

"No problem. You can use mine." She held out the bottle, then presented her back to him and lifted her hair off her shoulders with her free hand. "Would you mind? I can't reach. Then, I'll do you."

"Sure." Was that his voice cracking?

"This is some of Grandmother's special Lindon House sunscreen, guaranteed to 'have you a tropical bronze in one afternoon,' and at the same time cover you with an 'alluring fragrance to both men and women.'" Her laughter was skeptical.

He grunted. He didn't know how much more alluring

she could get without giving him heart failure. In two giant steps, he sprang forward and reached her side. Feeling like a bumbling teenager in the throes of a first crush, he took the bottle from her slender fingers, fumbled with the cap and emptied most of the liquid into his palm. "Oops." Uh-oh. She was going to be far more alluring that his blood pressure could tolerate.

"Problem?" She glanced over her shoulder.

"No. I—" He stared at the good-size puddle in his hand that was beginning to leak between his fingers. Okay. He was going to have to smear this stuff over her entire body and work on rubbing it in for the better part of the afternoon at this rate. Not that he minded that idea. No siree, Bob.

He held up his arm and the lotion ran to his elbow and began to drip. A large white splotch was forming on the linoleum floor at his feet. He laughed. This was ridiculous. "Well, actually, yes. I seem to have just a little too much of a good thing here."

Elizabeth tucked her chin to her shoulder and peered back to see what he was talking about. She giggled. "Well, at least the palm of your hand won't get burned."

"Thank heavens," he joked, "I hate when that happens."

"Here." She turned back around to face him and cupping his palm in hers, emptied half of the lotion into her own hand. Briskly rubbing her hands together, she spread the lotion evenly then began to apply it to his chest. "Go ahead," she urged, "get my back."

"Oh. Right. Sure." He stared down at her, transfixed, then obediently complying, he encircled her waist with his arms and began to run his slick palm over her smooth skin.

They stood face-to-face, smiling at each other. He took the step needed to better reach her back and, as he did so, her palms slid up over his biceps. Slowly, he massaged the lotion into her shoulder blades, then his fingers moved in firm circles up her spine to the base of her neck. A tiny moan of pleasure escaped her lips as he worked the sunscreen into these muscles and she leaned back and exposed her throat to him, her hair dangling over his wrist. His breathing became shallow. Her eyes fluttered shut, then opened just enough so that she could watch him watching her.

It would be so easy to kiss her, he thought, his gaze growing glassy. To take this relationship beyond a simple farce and into the realm of reality, right then and there. He'd kissed her before, in jest, for her family's benefit. But this would be different. And she would know it.

The intensity of their gaze was electric and the very air was alive with the current that snapped between them. He could feel their labored breathing forming a rhythmic cadence. Outside the pool house, a pair of birds squabbled. A light, balmy wind wafted through the breezeway, flirting with her hair as it draped over his wrists and caressing their heated flesh at the points where they connected. Her warm, silky-soft body seemed to meld to his as though they'd been born to fit together.

For the first time since he'd arrived, he suddenly wished for one of her wacky family members to arrive on the scene. Anybody would serve as a perfect excuse for him to lower his mouth to hers and give into the passion he felt igniting in his gut. But, they were alone and he couldn't. Not without somebody to perform for. He was her employee and, as such, physical displays of affection were part of the job.

Anything else might push her away. She'd made it clear, more than once, that the very idea of a relationship made her want to bolt. To run away and never come back. The very thought of losing her—the one woman who truly fit his idea of the perfect mate—just as he found her, struck a fear into his gut the magnitude of which he'd never experienced before in his life.

He convulsively pulled her closer, then took a deep, calming breath, let go and stepped back. There was a hint of a question and—maybe it was wishful thinking on his part—a flash of regret in her twilight blue gaze. It was one of the hardest things he'd ever done.

However, when this whole game was over and done with, it would be a different story.

Then, he wouldn't be in her employ.

This whole debacle would be behind them and he would be free and clear to begin courting her for real. To eventually bring her home to meet the family. Then, she would see firsthand how a wealthy family could love and support each other without reserve. And, hopefully she would begin to see that one didn't have to scrape along from paycheck to paycheck to be happy. Happiness was what they generated by simply being together.

He wiped what was left of the lotion in his hands on his swim trunks. "Ready?" He knew that if he didn't get out to that lake and go for a nice, chilling swim soon, he would spontaneously combust.

"I..." she blinked up at him, then smiled brightly. "Yes. Let's go."

Outside, the infinite Texas sky was a cloudless blue and the sun beat down promising a languid, relaxing afternoon, which was good, since Elizabeth was filled with sudden feelings of self-doubt and anxiety. She'd been so sure that Dakota was going to kiss her, this time, because he wanted to, and not because she was paying him to perform.

Her whole being was aching. Was she not his style?

Perhaps after getting to know her family he was leery of getting involved. And, could she blame him? She didn't want anything to do with that pack of scrapping magpies and she was a blood relative.

Slipping her sunglasses on to hide the depth of her confusion, she pushed her lips into a stoic smile and led Dakota away from the poolhouse and around the concrete deck of the swimming pool on the house side. The other side of the pool seemed to vanish over a steep embankment which overlooked the lake. From certain vantage points at pool level, the two separate bodies of water almost appeared to meld together as one long, azure body of water.

Flip-flops slapping, they descended the long staircase that ran from the poolhouse, straight down to the beach. From there, a long dock, built on pilings extended out into the crystal blue water. A few jet skis and both a sail and motorboat were moored to the dock. Water gently lapped against the side of their motorboat as they loaded their provisions and fishing gear.

Within an hour, they were lazily drifting in the shade of a willow grove, just off the shore of Victoria's small island. Surrounded by a lush green deciduous woods, their fishing lines bobbed in the water of this secluded cove. They lay side by side on the boat's comfortable leather seats, feet propped on coolers, the brims of their hats shading their eyes. Every once in a while, a catfish would jump, drawing their gaze and breaking the silence.

Elizabeth had used this time to become philosophical about Dakota's attraction. Or lack thereof. No doubt her family was part of his reticence to become involved. However, when this whole game was over and done with, that would be a different story. Then, he wouldn't be in her employ. And by then, she would be disinherited and just another simple gal from Hidden Valley. And, hopefully he would begin to see that scraping along from paycheck to paycheck on a ranch hand's wages could make her happy. Because to Elizabeth, happiness was what they generated by simply being together.

Having settled this matter in her mind, Elizabeth's pensive mood began to dissipate. It would all work out.

"Iced tea?" Elizabeth lifted the lid to her cooler and began to rummage.

From under the brim of his ball cap, Dakota peered at her and displayed his dimples. "I'm thirsty, yes." He held out his hand for the bottle.

"So. We should probably figure out what we're going to do about tonight."

"Yep." He popped the lid and took a swig of his tea.

Elizabeth popped the top to her own bottle and stared out over the crystalline blue of the lake. "Somehow or another, we have to figure out Victoria's Achilles' heel. We have to find the perfect thing that will make her mad enough to disown me, but won't permanently damage our relationship." She twisted her lips into a rueful smile. "In spite of everything, I really, really love Victoria. And, though she isn't big on mushy displays, I know she loves me. And wants me to be happy."

"She has a funny way of showing it."

Elizabeth rolled her gaze skyward. "True. Anyway, we have to come up with a plan. Fast. This is our last day here. Tomorrow, we head home and back to real life." She tried not to look as melancholy as she felt about this idyllic time with Dakota coming to an end.

"Okay. Victoria's Achilles' heel, huh?" Dakota shifted his position in the leather seat and gazed thoughtfully out to the horizon.

"Hmm. You know, there were a couple things in that

folder that she brought us last night, that really kind of stick out in my mind.''

Interest suddenly piqued, Elizabeth focused on him. ''What?''

''Well,'' Dakota held up a finger, ''first of all, she is very image conscious. As far as I can tell, image is everything to Lindon House.''

''That's true enough.''

He held up another finger, ''Second, she seems to be very hands-on when it comes to all of her business expenditures. Every giveaway, every promotion, every freebie has to be cleared through her. She's cautious. Doesn't take chances. Seems to play it a little safer than some other CEO's I've known.''

''You know a lot of CEO's?'' Elizabeth smiled.

His shrug was affable. ''Heard.''

Okay. She'd buy that. ''So she is image- and profit-oriented. How does that help us?''

A slow grin had the dimples bracketing the sides of his mouth in a most appealing manner. His enthusiasm was suddenly palpable. ''I think I have an idea that'll get you kicked out of Lindon House for good.''

Elizabeth sat up and leaned toward him, excitement bubbling into her throat. ''What?''

''I'll tell you in a second.'' He turned his attention from her and looked overboard.

''No, tell me now,'' she begged.

''Can't.''

''Why not?''

''I've got lunch on the line.''

Chapter Seven

Elizabeth felt as if she were hosting a ballet for butterflies in her stomach, such were the quiverings and flutterings within. As she hovered in the hallway just outside the Autumn Leaf Hotel's grand ballroom later that evening, she could hear the murmurings of the burgeoning crowd. The melodic strains of live classical music underscored the feel of refined culture that permeated the room.

Dakota was standing behind her, viewing the surroundings with interest. She groped for his fingers, and finding them, clutched and squeezed.

The ballroom was a study in elegance. The overhead lights had been dimmed and miles of tiny, twinkly lights adorned all nature of potted woodland flora. Up on stage, a black lacquer podium with a glass top awaited her use. Tall black art deco style vases flanked the podium and held bouquets of white lilies. From below, the glass floor was lit with a soft purple light that, when mixed with dry ice, gave the stage a magical quality.

Lindon House logos, in soft purple neon light provided

decoration to the backdrop of thick black velvet curtains that disguised a backstage area. In fact, everywhere the eye landed from the light patterns that shimmered on the wall, to the etching in the ice sculpture, the Lindon House logo was tastefully displayed.

Victoria had outdone herself this time. Everything screamed class. Money. Serenity.

People were still arriving, checking their wraps and bags and then following the red carpet into the ballroom. Dakota released her fingers and touched the back of her waist.

"Elizabeth."

"What?"

"We can't stand out here forever."

"Why not?"

"Come on now. This is going to be fun."

"If you say so." She had the sudden urge to bolt, but knew that she couldn't. Charles would simply hunt her down and guilt her into returning, just like he always did. Well, not anymore. She had to go through with this. She was running out of ideas and energy when it came to getting herself disinherited.

Dakota slipped his arm around her waist, gently steering and together they strolled into the ballroom.

Again, she was so thankful for his solid, reassuring presence. He looked incredibly handsome tonight. Though Charles's tux was a bit snug through the chest, Dakota looked far more suave and debonair than her brother ever would. It was almost as if Dakota had been born to this life. His purple cummerbund matched her shimmering purple evening gown and, for the moment, they looked just like Makeup Heiress Barbie and Country Club Ken out for an evening with the jet set. Anyone glancing at Dakota would most likely take him for just another wealthy playboy.

He steered her into line to check her wrap and she shot a glance at her wrist. "Okay," she whispered, and withdrew from her purse Victoria's duty list. She held it up for him to see. "According to this, we mingle and schmooze the crowd for about a half an hour."

His dimples bracketed the sides of his mouth. "Right."

"Then, you and I make our little presentation and introduce the products. Above all," she reminded him, "think image."

"And profit margin."

"Right. Let's mingle." She took a deep breath and glanced around at the somber expressions in line around them. Perhaps putting their plan into action would be a little more daunting than she'd originally thought. "You start."

He chuckled. "Chicken." To the high society couple standing behind them in the coat check line, Dakota turned and extended his hand. As he administered a vigorous handshake to each, he made enthusiastic introductions. "Howdy. I'm Dakota Brubaker, and this here is my better half, L.B. I run the ranch up at the Circle BO, and she waits tables down at Ned's Lonestar Grill. We're here to do a little favor for L.B.'s Nanna tonight."

"How do you do," came the reticent reply.

"We do all right. Say, you two look like beef eaters," Dakota rambled on, causing Elizabeth to smile in spite of her nerves, "if you ever get up Hidden Valley way, you oughta stop in at Ned's. The burgers are a little greasy, but shooee, I'm talkin' tasty eats." Dakota didn't let their nonplused expressions daunt him. "Say, now that we're friends, maybe later on at the dessert buffet after the show, we can sit together."

The strangers looked as if they'd rather kiss a rattlesnake.

And so it went as they moved through the coat check line and then through the crowd. As Dakota worked the room, Elizabeth followed and learned from the master.

"—taught L.B. here how to clean catfish today. Guts everywhere. But, she's a beginner, so you gotta cut her a little slack, right?"

"—drove the flatbed up here and made pretty good time. But then I always move a little faster when I'm not haulin' livestock."

"—when she inherits the Lindon House business from her Nanna. Then we got fun. I'm lookin' to buy us a rodeo."

Before long most of the room was buzzing about the two of them, and Elizabeth felt satisfied that they'd failed miserably as ambassadors for Victoria's sacred Lindon House image.

"Uh-oh." Her smile froze when she spotted Charles wending his way through the crowd toward them, Bernard in tow.

"What's wrong?"

"Charles is coming. With Bernard."

"In that case, let the festivities begin." Dakota's smile was so self-confident, that Elizabeth nearly forgot why she was afraid. Funny thing about Dakota Brubaker. When he was in the room her family lost the ability to cow her, and Bernard seemed more like an inconvenience, than any kind of threat.

A broad-girthed, fleshy-faced, neckless man, Bernard, looked as if he should be reclining in a hospital bed and wired to a cardiac monitor, rather than trotting along behind Charles. His rubicund complexion seemed to glow from the tips of his numerous chins to the top of his shiny pate, giving him the look of a thermometer that had been left in the fire overlong.

Charles was the first to speak as they reached Dakota and Elizabeth, which was a lucky thing, considering Bernard's winded state. "Bernard Mona, I'd like to introduce you to Dakota Brubaker. Elizabeth's…current husband."

"Current and only, Chuck. Try to keep that in mind. Hey, Bernie—" Dakota took Bernard's soft, damp palm in his own and tried to produce a handshake from the boneless appendage "—how ya doin'?"

"Very well, Brubaker," Bernard boomed, his blustery personality seeming to fill the room. "Charles, here, has told me a good deal about you."

"All good, I hope."

Bernard's too-loud laughter rang out. "Heard tell you're a cow puncher." The comment was meant to be condescending, but instead only emphasized how rugged and masculine Dakota was by comparison.

"Been known to punch a barnyard animal—" his gaze flicked to Charles, "or two in my time, yes." Dakota folded his arms across his chest in a gesture that Elizabeth noted had all of the women in the room watching him.

The subtle threat was not lost on Bernard and he hesitated slightly as he reached for Elizabeth. "Hello, Elizabeth." He dragged his fleshy lips across her cheek, then leaning back, tugged his snug jacket across his belly. "I was devastated to hear that you'd run off and married before we could give our love a chance."

Reaching out, Elizabeth grasped his hand and gave his sausage-like fingers a pat. "Oh, Bernard. You know you were always just too much man for me."

Before Bernard could analyze what exactly she meant by this comment, the lights flickered signaling the show was about to begin.

"We should probably get backstage," Dakota murmured, glancing at his watch. "According to Nanna's list, it's about time for you to do your hostess thing."

"Oh, boy." Nervously, she twisted her little wedding set on her finger. All the pieces were in place to execute the plan. It was a bit daring, but with any luck, should work.

Out there on Victoria's island, as they lay on the beach eating catfish cooked over an open fire and working out the logistics, it had seemed brilliant. Now Elizabeth wasn't so sure.

"Don't let Victoria down, Elizabeth." This was Charles's parting warning, as Dakota led her toward the stage.

"I won't," she assured him over her shoulder, and meant it. To allow Victoria to dictate her lifestyle would be to let her down. What she was about to do would set everyone free.

Backstage, in the dim light of a single bulb, Elizabeth and Dakota quickly changed into the props that Dakota had unearthed from his trunk, and a few that they rented from a costume shop on the way to the hotel that evening. Within minutes they were dressed like a couple of bronc busters waiting for the gate to swing open and the timer to begin.

"How do I look?" Elizabeth ran her clammy palms over the fringe on her vest, and then down over the rented chaps that rivaled his in bad taste.

"Like something from a really bad spaghetti Western. Love the belt buckle. It's nearly as big as mine."

"Thanks. You're lookin' pretty rhinestone cowboy yourself."

"Thanks." His straight white teeth flashed in the darkness. "You switch the music?"

"Yes." She nodded. "Feel like you've got a handle on the new speech?"

"Shucks, L.B., what we can't remember, we can ad-lib."

Elizabeth emitted some strangled laughter. "I like your confidence."

"Where's the product?"

"Out on stage. There's a little table. You can't miss it."

"Okay. I'm ready when you are."

"Then let's do it. Before I lose my nerve."

Elizabeth pushed the button on the CD player that was hooked to the ballroom's PA system and suddenly the room was filled with a raucous country-and-western music that would have brought tears of joy to Big Daddy's eyes. After several thundering minutes of heart-rending, hard luck lyrics about a man, his woman, her new man, his ex-wife and the endless regrets, Elizabeth throttled back the decibel level and gave Dakota the high sign. Together, she and Dakota burst through the black velvet drapes and ran out onto the stage, spurs jangling, whip cracking.

Though she hadn't really expected to be met with wild applause, the audience's stony silence was nearly as deafening as the music had been only moments before.

"Hello, everyone. I'm Elizabeth Derovencourt—er, Brubaker, Victoria Derovencourt's granddaughter. Victoria wanted me to come here tonight to talk to you about a new line of men's products that she has designed for the," she glanced over at Dakota, "common man, if you will."

On cue, Dakota scratched his chest—bare except for his denim vest and a longhorn bolo tie—and belched around the toothpick in his mouth.

Elizabeth couldn't see the audience all that well, but if the puckered expressions of the folks illuminated by the footlights were any indication, they were accomplishing their mission. A surge of adrenaline buoyed her and she forged ahead.

"It is the new Lindon House philosophy that skin care products have catered far too long to the man who has everything. The man who has nothing has been woefully overlooked. Right honey?"

Dakota's irreverent grin indicated that he couldn't give a rip about skin care. He winked at a socialite in the front row, and gave his pelvis a little swivel, eliciting a shocked gasp. "That's right, L.B."

"Folks, I'd like to introduce Dakota Brubaker to you as my husband. When we met, he knew nothing about beauty products for men. Right honey?"

"That's right, L.B." He moved up to the podium to stand next to Elizabeth and his voice was picked up by the PA. "Didn't think I deserved 'em. Me being the foreman of a ranch, I didn't think the hands—let alone the cattle— would care if I had smooth skin, or a fragrant aftershave. After all, they don't call it the Circle BO for nothing." He hooted at that, then affected mock sobriety. "When I started using Lindon House products, it was amazing how much my self-esteem improved. Since I started using the aftershave, I haven't violated my parole one single time. Right L.B.?"

"Right, honey."

The audience was staring, agog.

Dakota reached for a bottle of Victoria's debut after-shave. "They were gonna call this stuff *Billionaire*. But," he ripped off the label, wadded it and tossed it on the floor, "that name is a little off-putting to a simple guy like me. So, we decided to change our game plan and call it *Nuthin'* 'cuz this stuff goes on so smooth, it's almost like," he wiggled his eyes suggestively at the socialite in the front row, "wearin' nothin' at all." He poured out a handful and slapped it on his chest.

Elizabeth reached through the black velvet curtains and once again cranked the music.

"Yee haw!" Whooping to the beat, Dakota stripped off his vest and flung it at the dumbstruck crowd, then he began tearing the labels off the various products for men, and tossing the bare bottles into the audience. "And, the best part of wearin' *Nuthin'*?" he roared and cracked his whip. "Tell 'em, L.B.!"

"It's the price! It's…" she paused for dramatic effect, "*Nuthin'*. That's right folks," Elizabeth raised her voice to be heard above the throbbing music, "it's our gift for the man who has nothing!"

"And," Dakota tugged the microphone away from Elizabeth to be heard over the growing din of the crowd, "before we are done this evening, we are going to give away a whole lotta *Nuthin'*." After that, we're gonna award our best customer, Bernard Mona, of Monaco's department store, the 'Thanks for *Nuthin'*' award."

The women in the front row began to fan themselves with their programs. The hue and cry of the mob began to escalate.

Dakota grinned at Elizabeth. "I think it's beginning to work," he mouthed. "Chuck's leaving."

Elizabeth watched her brother stride angrily out of the room and had mixed emotions. For, as much as she desperately wanted to be free to live her own life, she wished they hadn't pushed her to this.

"I don't believe this."

Elizabeth dragged her gaze from Dakota's and stared in shock at the frenzied crowd as they clambered to fill their arms with bottles of *Nuthin'*. At some point during their demonstration, the audience had turned the corner and joined them in the insanity.

One, then two, and three—and more—at a time, people were catching on to the brilliant advertising gimmick, and loving it. A smattering of applause turned into a full-scale riot. Suddenly dignified matrons and their stuffed-shirt husbands were on the bandwagon, joining the hue and cry to provide the man who has nuthin' with…*Nuthin'*.

Buyers from all the major department stores couldn't seem to put in their orders fast enough for not only *Nuthin'*, but all of the complementary products that went with it. Never before had anybody heard of a company pulling such an amazing coup.

No wonder Victoria Derovencourt wanted her granddaughter and her husband to take over the company. Together, they were golden.

Soon, several journalists for major society rags were heard to say, Lindon House would, without a doubt, be more wildly successful than ever before. And all thanks to *Nuthin'*. By tomorrow morning, the wonderful news would make all the papers and talk shows.

In a depressed fog, Elizabeth thanked the crowd for attending. Behind the stage, she shucked her costume down to a simple pair of jeans and a western top and then, without waiting for Dakota, ran out of the double glass doors that led to one of the many patio areas just beyond the ballroom.

Dakota followed, and found her sitting on the broad, concrete edge of a fountain. It was difficult to tell which was spilling more water, the shell-wearing mermaid sitting in the center of the fountain, or the jeans clad woman sitting beside.

The beautiful patio was surrounded by a concrete railing supported by fat, decorative balustrades. Ornate lampposts flanked a massive staircase that led to the rolling lawn below. Several water gardens, imbedded in the patio, were filled with fish and lily pads and the full moon was reflected in the rippling water.

Slowly, Dakota approached the fountain and took a seat next to her on the concrete ledge. Without a word, she leaned toward him and nestled her head against his shoulder. He handed her the handkerchief he carried in his hip pocket. As she dabbed at her eyes and nose, he circled her shoulders with his arm. In silence they sat listening to the soothing murmurings of the fountain.

Finally, she rallied and sent him a beleaguered look. "Why is it that everything I touch turns to gold?"

It was a rhetorical question, but he groped for an answer that would satisfy. His gaze traveled to the place where her hand rested lightly on his knee and he thought about his own vast fortune. Luckily, she had no idea of the irony of her words.

"It's a curse?" he joshed, in an effort to keep things light. To keep his mind off that inevitable day when she would discover the truth about him.

"Very funny." She sighed. "As hard as I try, I can't seem to get away from the stupid money. You have no idea how frustrating it is. Lucky you. You'll never have to worry about the pain in the neck that being rich can cause."

He studied her plaintive expression. "Do you really want to get away from money that badly?"

"Yes!" Eyes sparking, tone vehement, she waved his handkerchief at the brightly lit ballroom windows and the frenzy beyond. "Just look at those people in there. The emperor has no clothes, yet they are only too happy to follow the latest craze. *Nuthin'*. What a crock."

"I don't know. I think it's kinda catchy."

"Don't go and make me laugh. I'm mad and I want to stay that way. Do you realize that we have just proved Victoria right? She is going to be thrilled when she finds out what we have done for both her image, and her profit index. Now, she'll be worse than relentless. I'll never be able to hold out against her now."

As she flopped back against him, Dakota had to force himself not to pull her into his arms and kiss her senseless. She wasn't ready to be a real couple, he reminded himself yet again. She was too busy sorting out her past, to jump into a future with him. He had to let her work this out at her own pace.

But it was hard.

Fear was making him desperate. What would happen when she discovered his secret? Would she hate him? Run away, as she had from her own family? This whole thing was getting so damn complicated.

He peered through the shadows down into her face, memorizing again, the details he already knew by heart. The moon's soft glow gave her a mystical beauty that took his breath away. With the pad of his thumb, he traced the pout of her lower lip. An incredible possessiveness consumed him as he sat absorbing her essence. Deep in his soul, he knew that she was his other half. Without her, his future had no meaning at all. And, until she figured that out for herself, he was doomed to a life of uncertainty.

She smiled against his thumb and her low giggle drew his attention and made him temporarily forget his worries. "What's so funny?"

"Oh," she shrugged, "the whole thing. I really thought I was going to lose it when you were mingling. The look on those people's faces was priceless when you said some of the stuff you said. Victoria would kill you if she knew."

He schooled his face into a mask of innocence. "What'd I say that was so bad?"

"How about that *Billionaire* sounded like bunion air, for one thing."

"Well, doesn't it?"

"I guess." Her shoulders bobbed with her mirth. "Whatever that is."

He grinned. "It's a cross between an old shoe and an onion."

"Oh, please." This set her into another gale of giggles that had her flopping against him in glee. "Then when you started off on that tangent about wanting to create Lindon House products for livestock—" She patted his chest with a limp hand and her eyes scrunched shut.

He feigned wounded feelings. "I think it's an over-looked market."

They laughed together for a long, tension releasing moment, enjoying each other's company and sense of humor.

A sound from the ballroom's glass doors jarred him slightly from his reverie and in his peripheral vision he noticed some movement over Elizabeth's shoulder. Tearing his gaze from her face, he glanced up, then heaved an annoyed sigh.

For pity's sake.

His head swung back and leaning toward her, brought his mouth close to her ear. "Bernard is watching us from the ballroom." A jaw muscle twitched in aggravation.

Her laughter mellowed into a slow smile and with a teasing lift of her brow she said, "Then what are you waiting for, husband? Kiss me."

Dakota didn't need to be told twice. Even though this kiss was only a means to an end, he threw himself into the role, heart and soul. Cupping her cheeks in his hands, he angled her mouth just beneath his and held back just a fraction to make sure this is what she really wanted. Though their mouths were not yet touching, their breathing became ragged and her shallow breath tickled his lips. Eyes flashing, he asked without words, just to make sure she knew what she wanted, and she arched against him in answer.

Their noses bumped and settled into position as his mouth sought, and claimed hers. A low groan emanated in his throat as she wound her arms up around his neck. Time suspended. His fingertips probed the heated spot where their mouths melded, then traced the column of her throat. From there, his hands slipped around her waist and he pulled her against his chest and buried his hands in the silky cloud of her hair.

For a brief moment, he managed to feel just the tiniest bit sorry for old Bernard. But the feelings of pity passed just as soon as they came. Bernard had his chance.

Elizabeth was his now, he thought possessively. Didn't matter that she wasn't legally his wife. That was simply a matter of semantics in his mind. Soon enough, they would be married for real.

Even if he had to renounce his own inheritance and live the rest of his life as a poor man to make it so.

Chapter Eight

"You're kidding, right?"

"No." Morose, Elizabeth shook her head. "Victoria said, and I'm quoting here, 'I'm going to go home to Hidden Valley with you, tomorrow morning. I'll be staying with you in your bunk bed.'"

"Bunk bed?" Completely nonplused, Dakota stared. "Uh, she must mean bunkhouse. Not bunk bed."

"Whatever."

"There's a pretty big difference."

"She doesn't seem to care."

"I can't believe it." Hand on the doorknob to her suite, Dakota stepped back to admit Elizabeth.

"Believe it. She's not big on joking around."

As she brushed past, Dakota shut the door and, deftly aiming the remote over his shoulder, muted the sound on the television. It appeared to Elizabeth that he'd been waylaid by the sports channel on his way to his bedroom to change out of his tuxedo.

His jacket lay over the back of the sofa and tossing her

wrap on top of that, Elizabeth kicked off her pumps and sank to the cushion. "I think she's calling our bluff."

"What do you want to do?"

"Well…" Cringing, Elizabeth looked up at him, then dropped her head into her hands. A slow, heavy sigh escaped her lips as she propped her elbows on her knees and pressed her fingertips to her throbbing temples. "Oh, Dakota, I really hate to impose on you any more than I already have, but I don't really know what else to do. I'll make it worth your while, I swear." She braced herself for Dakota's refusal. "So what do you say? Want to stay married for a few more days?"

Angling her head, she smiled weakly and watched Dakota sink down beside her on the sofa. He was clearly shell-shocked. His grin was cockeyed as he stared unseeing at the soundless sports on the television screen. Elizabeth guessed he must be trying to figure a way out of this mess. And who could blame him? Poor guy. One minute, he'd been a happy-go-lucky single guy, eating his lunch down at the diner and minding his own business, and the next minute, he'd been drafted into the family from hell's furnace room.

For a moment, Elizabeth reflected on the brief conversation she'd had with Victoria in the parlor, only a few minutes before.

When she and Dakota had come home from the Lindon House preview it had been nearly midnight and her family—with the lone exception of Victoria—had already retired for the night. The older woman had been dozing in a club chair in the den just off the grand foyer when they'd arrived. Jolted to wakefulness, Victoria had rubbed her eyes, adjusted her glasses and after a few cryptic pleasantries, demanded a moment of Elizabeth's time.

Alone.

In keeping with his character, Dakota—before he bounded out of the room—planted a noisy kiss on the tip of the old matriarch's beakish nose. Too flabbergasted and fiery-cheeked to protest, Victoria put on a mock show of disdain and turned her attention to her granddaughter, whom she grilled for the details of the preview.

"Charles filled me in on everything that happened tonight. I *knew* you could do it," she crowed, gloating at the news of the unmitigated success. "Even when you don't want to be, you are a natural. Just think of the things you could accomplish, given the proper attitude. *Nuthin'*. Why didn't I think of that? Brilliant."

"It wasn't my idea, it was Dakota's."

"Fluke." Victoria sniffed. "Anyway, you had the foresight to follow it through. You are a born leader."

"In spite of tonight's success, Grandmother, I don't want to run the company."

"What? But why not?" Peeved, Victoria grabbed her cane from where it was propped beside her chair and smacked it on the floor. "You want to lead the alluring lifestyles of the impoverished and infamous. I simply do not understand you!" Gnarled knuckles whitened as she gripped the cane and took a long, deep breath, then blew it out. "But to show that I'm flexible, I'm going to try."

The tiny hairs on the back of Elizabeth's neck had stood at attention at the unusually benign look on her grandmother's face. "Try what?"

"To understand you. To see things from your point of view."

"What do you mean?"

"Well, I've been giving this whole situation some thought tonight, and I've made a decision."

"Uh-oh. What decision?"

"When you and your...Dakota person," Victoria waved

her hand dismissively, "leave to return home to your bunk bed in the morning, I'll be coming with you."

Check and mate.

Elizabeth was speechless.

Victoria was going to Hidden Valley?

After a few last edicts and particulars from Victoria, the discussion was over. The old woman—tuning out Elizabeth's every protest—had summoned a servant to assist her and had wobbled up the massive staircase and off to her room to pack.

Fearing Dakota's reaction, Elizabeth rushed back to her suite to face him. And, just as she'd anticipated, he looked as thunderstruck as she felt.

He flopped back against the sofa and ran a hand over his jaw as he spoke. "Did she…uh, say how long she wants to stay?"

She gave her head a quick bob and squeezed her eyes tightly shut. "A week?" She peeked at him through one eye to gauge his reaction.

"A…week? Out at the ranch?" Jaw slack, his tone was incredulous.

This was not good. She was beginning to wear on his good nature, she could tell. But she had no choice. They'd come too far to bail out now.

"I can't imagine she would last that long," she hastened to assure him. "Especially, if we make her miserable enough. Without somebody to wait on her hand and foot, catering to her special diet needs, not to mention all of her ergonomically correct and adjustable furniture, plus all of her medical paraphernalia, well, I'd be surprised if she wasn't speeding back to Lindon House by lunchtime."

"Do you have any idea why she wants to do this?"

Elizabeth cleared her throat. "She mentioned something

about getting in touch with the charming rusticity of your bunk bed.''

"House. Bunk*house*.'' Dakota propped his lanky legs on the coffee table. Elbows high, he leaned back and cradled the back of his head in his hands. "Yeah, right. What's the real reason? Has she gone and adopted the old if-you-can't-beat-'em-join-'em theory?''

"Not Victoria. If she can't beat you, she has one of the servants do it for her.''

Dakota laughed.

"Anyway,'' Elizabeth shrugged, "she claims that the reason she wants to come stay with us is to find out what it is that I find so fascinating about being poor.''

"And, besides me,'' a slow grin tipped his lips and he studied her intently, "what *do* you find so fascinating about being poor?''

Lately, he was the number one fascination, but she could hardly admit to that. "For one thing, I want to live in the real world, not some fantasy bubble. I'm sick of missing out on the simple pleasures. And, for another, when you have to work hard for what you get, you appreciate it that much more.''

"You'd have to work hard, if you took over Lindon House for your grandmother.''

"True. But there is the greed factor. I want to be part of a family of people who love each other for what they are and not what they have.''

"Ahh.'' He scratched his jaw and his whiskers made a pleasant rasping sound. "So you would consider living with a rich family, if money was not a factor? If they loved you for who you were?''

Elizabeth sighed. She wished he'd stop trying to talk her out of being poor. "There is no such family.''

"There might be.''

"Not my family. Not in this lifetime."

"Don't be so sure."

It was a nice fairy tale, but Elizabeth knew better. The fact that Dakota was trying to make her see that she could be happy as a corporate mogul depressed her. That they were not thinking on the same lines for her future was apparent. She leaned back into her corner of the sofa and crossed her arms over her stomach to ease the sudden pang she felt there. Blessedly, he was unaware of her yearning for a life of austere simplicity with him, and stretching, he yawned and settled into a more comfortable position himself.

"You know, I don't get why she'd want to travel all the way to Hidden Valley with us, especially since she called you here to her virtual deathbed. Isn't she too sick to make this trip?"

"I think we both know the answer to that," Elizabeth said, ruefully. "Even so, when I approached the subject of her delicate health, she shouted that she can die in Hidden Valley as easily as she can here at home."

With a tilt of his head, he gave a she-has-a-point lift of his brow.

"And, of course," Elizabeth continued, "she can spy on us much better in person, than she can sending my brother to do the job."

"Spy?"

"Yes. To see if we are really married. Really living together."

His dimples slowly appeared. "That could be a problem."

"I know." Elizabeth moaned. "She's going to see from the moment she walks into your place that I don't live there."

Dakota held up a hand. "Now don't panic. I'm sure we can think of something."

"I tried to talk her out of going, Dakota, but she wouldn't take no for an answer. You know how stubborn she can be."

"Yep."

Laughing, he stripped off his purple bow tie and tossed it on the coffee table. The cummerbund followed and after that, the cuff links. Powerful, tan forearms were revealed as he deftly rolled up his sleeves and, as Elizabeth watched his smooth motions, her mouth went dry.

To distract herself, she curled her legs under her body and concentrated on sitting still and not following through with the overwhelming desire she had to crawl into his lap and hide from the big, complicated world.

"Toss me the phone, will ya, honey?"

Though he used the endearment without thinking, her heart did a little flip beneath her breast. She reached for the wireless that lay next to the lamp on the end table. "Who are you going to call at this time of night?"

"The troops. We're going to need some help if we're going to pull the rest of this charade off."

Relief so sweet she could eat it for dessert, flooded her being. "You're going to help?"

"Sure." He looked surprised that she'd even ask. "We've gone this far."

"Oh, thank you, thank you," she whispered. "I owe you."

"No biggie." He held up a hand and turned his attention to the phone. "Fuzzy? That you? Did I wake you? No? Good. Listen, I need you and Red to do me a favor. A small one. For me and Elizabeth. Yeah. She's right here." He exhaled noisily and rolled his eyes. "Shut up. Tell Red to shut up, too."

Elizabeth couldn't begin to guess what was being said on the other end of the line, but the pained expression on Dakota's face made her think that might be a good thing.

"Okay, here's the deal. You guys need to go over to Elizabeth's place and pack up some of her stuff and move it into my bunkhouse. She's going to be staying with me. Oh, you're a regular laugh riot." Dakota slowly shook his head. "No, it's not what you think. Her grandmother is going to be staying with us, too. We need to make it look like Elizabeth lives there. Like she's lived there for a long time. Yes. Very funny. Listen up. I can't go into that right now. Right. I'll tell you later."

The corners of his eyes crinkled as he smiled at her and patted her leg.

"Tell Montana I said to clear out. I don't care. He can stay with you and Red. Why not? It's only for a week, it's not like it's gonna kill any of you."

His expression turned apologetic and he covered the mouthpiece with his hand. "Do you have a spare key to your trailer?"

She nodded.

"Where do you keep it?"

"Under the welcome mat."

His narrowed gaze was loaded with censure. "That's dangerous. I don't want you to keep it there anymore."

"Yes, sir." A tiny smile tugged at her lips. The fact that he cared for her well-being took the indignation out of her sails.

"Fuzzy. I need you to go get a pencil and write down the directions to Elizabeth's place." As he waited for Fuzzy to accomplish this task, he tugged his shirttails from his waistband and slowly began to unbutton his shirt. After he gave detailed directions, he said, "Get the key from under her mat. Yeah, I know. I already told her not to do it anymore." He winked at her.

"Go inside and get a bunch of her stuff. Hell, I don't know. Clothes and stuff. Anything that looks girlie. Put it in some boxes and bring it back to my place and spread it around and make it look like she lives there. Pictures on the wall? Sure. I don't care. Flowers? Whatever. Just do your best."

Again, he turned his attention to her. "Anything special you want 'em to pick up for you?"

She swallowed past the growing lump in her throat. They were all so sweet to help her out this way. She would have to do something really nice for all of them. "Uh, let's see. I have a book on my nightstand, and…oh, I'm going to need my work clothes. My uniform is in the dryer and my shoes are the ugly white ones by the bed. My car keys are hanging over the microwave in the kitchen, if someone wants to bring my car."

"Good idea. You hear that Fuzzy? Good." Lazily, he rubbed his chest with his fingertips and Elizabeth swallowed. "Okay, we should be there by—" he shot an inquisitive glance at Elizabeth.

Elizabeth tore her eyes from the smooth, tanned muscles that peeked through the unbuttoned placket of his shirt and thought for a moment. She hunched her shoulders and let them fall. "I guess we could be there by midmorning."

"Hear that? Okay, see you then. And, remember, I'm a married man. Spread the word." He sighed. "You idiots knock it off."

He hung up the phone and his sexy smile had her heart pounding. "Well, it's official. You live with me."

Even though it would only be for a few short days, it was still a dream come true. Elizabeth clasped her hands together and willed her pulse to slow. It wouldn't do to jump up and down and shout for joy. "I can't thank you enough."

"My pleasure."

"You may not feel that way when Victoria gets down there and starts interfering in our marriage and making life a living hell."

"Well, we'll just have to stay on the same wavelength, then, huh?"

Elizabeth grinned. "Want to go downstairs and raid the pantry with me and tell me how we're going to do that? I'm hungry."

"Excellent idea. I'm starved."

Pant legs rolled to the knees, Dakota dangled his feet in the backyard hot tub as he and Elizabeth polished off what was left of a bag of Oreo cookies and a quart of milk. Her shimmering purple gown was pushed up to her thighs and her bare legs disappeared into the steaming bubbles. The moon had traveled in the sky and was smaller and higher, but no less bright. Side by side they sat in the warm evening breeze and laughed and talked and got to know each other better.

"I had fun today." Elizabeth darted a shy glance at him.

"Me, too." Although, Dakota thought, tomorrow promised to be even better. He still couldn't believe his good fortune. A powerful surge of adrenaline flowed through his body, giving him a heady sense of well-being. Elizabeth was moving in. This was just the break he needed. Now, instead of dropping her off at her place and hoping against hope for another date sometime next weekend, she was going to move into his place.

Lock, stock and...Victoria.

But so what? So, the cranky old woman was part of the deal. No problem. At this point, he was ready to do anything to prove how much he cared. Hopefully, his brothers and those boneheads he worked with would cooperate and not blow their cover.

Elizabeth held up the empty cookie package and frowning, crumpled it up. "All gone."

"That's all we've eaten since lunch. I'm still hungry."

"Me, too."

"Probably too late to go fishin'."

"Probably. By the way, you barbecue a mean catfish. I don't think I've ever tasted anything so delicious."

Dakota buffed his nails on his open shirt. "It's a knack. In our family, barbecue is a sacred ritual passed from father to son. Never met a woman who could barbecue worth beans."

Mouth dropping, eyes narrowing, Elizabeth poked him in the chest with her finger. "Them's fightin' words, buddy boy."

"You threatening to barbecue for me?"

"I might be."

"You're on."

Her laughter bubbled along with the hot tub's jets. "Wouldn't Victoria love that?"

He chuckled. "Oh, I expect she's got all kinds of surprises waiting for her in the next few days."

"Mmm. What do you say we take her to Ned's for lunch tomorrow?"

"Oh, yeah. A sloppy old Longhorn burger might be just what the doctor ordered."

"Is it a date then?"

Dakota nodded. Victoria or no, this was shaping up to be the best week he'd ever had. "It's a date."

An hour later, in the wee hours of the morning, Elizabeth bid Dakota good-night and slipped into her own room. As she changed into her nightgown and went through the nightly rituals of brushing her hair and teeth and washing her face, she could hear Dakota in his bathroom doing the same. The most wonderful sense of home seemed to transform her formerly sterile suite. It was so incredibly nice to have someone with whom to share even life's most mundane chores.

She snapped off the bathroom light and padded into her room. Moving to her door, she cracked it open so that she wouldn't feel so far away from him during the night. She paused for a moment in the archway to her room and stared at his closed door, vacillating.

Try as she might, an excuse to go visit him eluded her. It was well after midnight. It had been a long and grueling day. No doubt, Dakota was dog dead tired. After he'd talked to Fuzzy on the phone, they'd packed and made lists and plans before they'd soaked their feet in the hot tub. They were as ready as two people could be, for Victoria's visit.

Elizabeth supposed that knocking on his door and requesting a practice good-night kiss, for Victoria's sake, of course, would be a little transparent on her part. Not to mention selfish. This weekend had kept him hopping. She was going to have to pay him overtime as it was. He deserved some sleep.

She leaned against the marble pillar and listened to the homey little sounds of a man preparing for bed. The curiosity threatened to drive her mad. What was he doing in there? Her mind drifted to the way he'd worn his tuxedo shirt unbuttoned and rolled up the sleeves. Such a powerful chest and muscular arms. They didn't grow men like that in her social circle. Strong, sexy men who knew their own minds. Who knew about hard work in the real world. Who knew how to make a woman feel like a woman, and not an end to a means.

A long, slow sigh from deep within her lungs blew past her lips.

Arms wound round the pillar, she pressed her face against its smooth marble surface, cooling the fever that burned as she thought of the kiss they'd shared earlier out at the fountain. Even now she could feel his soft lips traverse the column of her throat, and goose bumps, like a flash fire, rippled across her heated flesh. Had he been as affected as she had?

Probably not. He'd made a point of telling her on the way over here that he was happy being single. If he really cared for her, he'd kiss her when there was no one to watch. Like now.

Now.

She willed him into the hallway to discover her standing there, but of course, that didn't work. For too long she stood thinking of ways to approach him, and the spontaneity evaporated. So, she turned and went back to her bed.

Once she'd slipped between the sheets, she lay still and, listening intently, identified the sounds of him changing from his formal clothes into heaven only knew what. Did he wear pajamas? He was humming a tuneless ditty. His door opened and she froze where she lay under her covers. Seconds ticked by. Then, his footfalls receded back into his room. A short while later, his bed creaked as he climbed in and found a position that made him comfortable.

A bittersweet longing filled her. All her life, she'd dreamed of a loving, cozy relationship with a special man. This weekend was giving her just the taste of what she'd been missing out on all these years.

While it was true that she'd only known Dakota for two

months, it felt like a lifetime. It was so easy to imagine that they'd been performing these routines together for years.

Funny. From the beginning, she'd liked Dakota and had been attracted to his rough-and-tumble good looks. But, over the last few days, her feelings had intensified to the point where she was beginning to believe that he was the one.

The one.

The one who could convince her to give up a lifetime of trying to wrangle out of a commitment, for a lifetime of commitment.

From the next room, the deep, even sound of his sleep was a melody to her ears. Drowsy, she nestled down and soon, the slow easy rhythm of his slumber lulled her off to sleep.

The next morning, on her way back from the dining room—where she'd tried once again, unsuccessfully, to talk Victoria out of going to Hidden Valley with them—Elizabeth found Dakota stacking their bags in the hallway, just outside the doors of her suite. His hair, the color of honey in a jar on a sunny window ledge, was still damp from the shower. The ends curled slightly at his nape and Elizabeth longed to reach out and smooth them with her fingertips.

Seeming to sense her approach, he turned and smiled, his chiseled lips revealing his beautiful pearly whites. "There you are." He pushed the fingers of both hands through his damp hair, his T-shirt stretching across his broad chest, his biceps flexing as he did so. "I wondered where you'd disappeared to."

"I was, uh—" Her eyes glazed over as he planted his hands on his narrow hips. Hooking his thumbs through the faded denim belt loops of his jeans, he stood smiling expectantly at her, waiting for her to continue. She blinked, trying to remember where she'd been only moments ago. "Oh, uh, I was just downstairs trying to talk some sense into Victoria."

He cocked his head. "How'd it go?"

"Well, she really didn't listen."

"Uh-oh."

"Yeah." Elizabeth leaned against the hall wall and watched as he dropped to his haunches to zip up the zippers and fasten the Velcro tabs on his bags. She waved a limp hand toward the broad landing of the curved double staircase. "For once, as you can hear, my family agrees with me."

Angry voices echoed up the stairs and down the hall to where they stood. Charles and Ashby were doing their best to convince Victoria that this trip was folly, and Victoria was telling them in no uncertain terms just what they could do with their concern.

Dakota rocked back on his heels and chuckled. "She's stubborn all right. It's why she's so successful in business."

"I guess."

Hands to knees, he pushed himself upright and Elizabeth followed him into the suite and closed the door behind her to shut out the noise.

Dakota ambled to the sofa and picked up his Stetson and eased it into place on his head. Tiny lines crinkled at the corners of his eyes as he turned his gaze on her. Her heart did a little flip. He was the quintessential cowboy, ruggedly built with rangy muscles and sun-kissed good looks. Not wanting him to see how breathless he made her, she tore her gaze from his compelling physique and allowed it to travel around the room in a pretense of searching for anything they may have left behind since she didn't plan on returning anytime soon. "Are we all packed and ready to go?"

He gave his head a slow bob and lazily ran a hand over his upper arm. "Far as I can tell. I left Charles's clothes hanging in the closet to be dry-cleaned." Creases bracketed the sides of his mouth. "Thought about stealing some towels, just to give Nanna some more fuel for her fire, but they wouldn't fit in my bag."

Elizabeth giggled at the ludicrous idea. She loved his easy humor. Luckily, a knock sounded at her door, preventing her from standing there and going into another googlie-eyed trance over his beauty.

"I'll get it," she grumbled. "Just my luck, it'll be Publisher's Clearing House coming to tell me I won ten million dollars."

His baritone laughter rumbled from deep within his chest. Before she could move to the door, he grasped her arm.

"No, wait, wait," he whispered. "Come here." He tugged her into his embrace, curling his body around her and resting his forehead against her own. His warm, minty breath tickled her lips as he spoke. "Now this is more like it." Raising his voice, he called out to the person beyond the door. "Come on in, it's unlocked." Then, he settled his lips over hers in the softest of featherlight kisses. Weak in the knees, she clutched his shoulders.

"Ah-hem." Simon's voice, steeped in embarrassment, reached them. "I've come to take your bags downstairs. Sir. Ma'am."

"Thank you, Simon," Elizabeth finally gasped, when Dakota released her mouth. With one hand cradling her waist, Dakota fished a dollar bill out of his snug jeans pocket with the other and held it out to Simon, not bothering to tear his piercing gaze from her eyes.

"Here you go, buddy. Everything is right outside the door for you."

Simon sighed and took the bill. "Sir."

As Simon backed out of the suite, Dakota took the opportunity to impress him with his husbandly ardor and, crushing Elizabeth to his body, pressed his mouth to the hollow spot that throbbed at her throat. Elizabeth arched against him, reveling in the wonder of his touch. He smelled fresh and clean from his shower, and just a little bit like *Nuthin'*. A tiny whimper escaped her lips. She had to admit, Victoria knew what she was doing with her men's skin care products. This stuff made her want to bury her face in Dakota's neck and never leave.

Once again, Simon cleared his throat. "Er, excuse me. Madam Derovencourt has ordered me to bring her limousine around and will be ready to depart for Hidden Valley shortly."

"Fine, fine, whatever." Irritated at the interruption, Dakota waved Simon off. "Tell her we'll be there in a minute."

Elizabeth giggled as he noisily nuzzled her neck, oblivious to the fact that Simon was gone and he could stop performing.

"Mmm," Dakota murmured, "I could stay here all day."

"But we can't."

"I know. Nanna's waiting."

Elizabeth leaned back in his arms and looked up into his handsome face. "I think I have a little stage fright. How are we going to keep Victoria from snooping around and somehow discovering that we're not married?"

"We're going to have to keep her really, really busy."

"What do you have in mind?"

"Well, we'll just have to play it by ear. Tonight, maybe you could barbecue for us while I watch sports on TV. That'll look realistic." He grinned and wiggled his eyebrows. "Then, of course, it'll be bedtime."

Elizabeth swallowed. "Where will Victoria sleep?"

"I'll make sure she has her own bunk bedroom," he teased. "And you and I? We'll figure something out in my room." With gentle fingers, he reached up and pulled a strand of hair away from her mouth.

"Oh. Okay."

"Then, since I'll have to get some catch-up work done in the morning, maybe I'll have Fuzzy and Red give you two the official tour of the ranch."

"The official tour?"

"Oh sure. We'll put her in my uncle's old jeep and show her the back ten or twenty thousand."

"Thousand?"

"Acres." He dimpled.

Elizabeth traced these indentations with her fingers and smiled flirtatiously at him. "Sounds like fun."

"Oh, yeah."

"Dakota…"

"Hmm?"

"What if it doesn't work?"

He stroked her hair and brushed his lips lightly against hers. "Then, I guess we're just going to have to get married."

Elizabeth's pulse caught. She knew he was just teasing. But she also knew that if he were serious, she'd follow him to the courthouse this very second. Nothing would make Elizabeth happier than spending the rest of her life as Mrs. Dakota Brubaker.

Nuthin'.

Chapter Nine

"So this is it." Elizabeth pressed her face to the passenger door window. Eagerly, she drank in the sights as—shortly after noon—Dakota bumped over the dusty road that led through the back sections of the ranch toward his bunkhouse. The delightful grouping of cabins lay just ahead under the shade of a thick stand of willows and live oaks. A good-size pond, situated in the center of this backwoods neighborhood for cowboys, reflected a deep, sea blue summer sky through which cottony clouds silently floated over Dakota's family ranch.

It was heaven.

"Yep." Dakota slowed and checked the rearview mirror for Simon and Victoria, who jounced along behind in the limousine, obscured from sight by the creamy yellow dust blizzard. "This is it."

A feeling of sublime déjà vu niggled at Elizabeth.

These little cabins were exactly what she pictured in her mind's eye, whenever she fantasized about her future home. She could just see one of these simple houses fixed up the way she liked it, with her favorite chair on the sprawling porch and a stack of novels and a pitcher of iced tea nearby. A little gardening would have fragrant roses climbing an arbor that Dakota would build to straddle the front walkway. From there, a picket fence would be perfect around the perimeter of property.

Her gaze shifted. Behind the cabins, off in the distance, a slight breeze rippled through vast oceans of grain. Like long-horned ships, cud-chewing bovine herds voyaged from port to port, pasture to pasture.

Elizabeth felt as though she were finally returning home, after a long, miserable absence. Grasping the old turn-crank handle on the passenger door, she unrolled the window to inhale the delightful mix of dust and heat and Texas ranch land. The sound of bawling cattle off in the distance blew into the cab with the breezes, and Elizabeth knew a contentment that she'd never known before.

"Where does your uncle live?"

"He lives in the main house, a mile or two from here, on the other side of the stables. I took the back driveway, because it's…closer." Something in his voice made Elizabeth look back over her shoulder at him.

"Are we going to go visit him? I'd love to meet more of your family."

He flexed his hands on the steering wheel and shrugged. "Nah. Not yet. I don't want to overwhelm Victoria right away."

"Oh." Elizabeth smiled brightly to mask her disappointment. "You're probably right. Soon, though, okay?"

"Sure." An enigmatic look crossed his face and his gaze was piercing as he studied her. "You're going to meet the whole family sooner or later."

Elizabeth draped her elbows over the edge of the low-ered window and peered into the rearview mirror on her door. The limousine, once a sleek, shiny black, now resembled an overripe banana. In the backseat, she could see Victoria hanging onto her hat and looking about, mouth agape. Simon too, appeared to be feeling the stress as he dodged potholes and stray cattle without the proper shock absorbers.

As Dakota pulled the flatbed to a stop along the gravel road in front of the bunkhouses, the ranch hands all came bounding out of a building marked Circle BO Ranch Offices to greet them. Every last one of them was waving and beaming like a pack of grinning idiots. It was obvious that this charade was the most fun any of these guys had had in a long time. Dakota cut the engine and, while it coughed and shimmied, he pointed out each ranch hand and quickly told Elizabeth their names.

"That old geezer with the whiskers and the canary eatin' grin, that's Fuzzy. The guy standing next to him with the red face and hair, that's Red. Over there is Sly, Hunt, Colt and," he pointed out a man who was his spitting image, "last but not least, my brother and your brother-in-law, Montana. Remember to pretend you know them. Hopefully, they'll do the same."

Maneuvering around the flatbed, Simon pulled the limousine ahead and began the arduous process of parallel parking between the truck and an old jeep that was sitting a bit further up the road in front of the offices. Dakota hadn't left Simon much space, and an inch at a time the limousine lurched back and forth. Energetically, he spun the wheel this way and that, earning every penny of the dollar that Dakota planned to send his way.

Inside the cab of the flatbed, Elizabeth turned to Dakota. Entranced, her eyes fairly glowed and her face was transformed as she looked around the place Dakota called home.

"I can see why you love your job so much. Living here would be a dream come true."

Dakota watched her gaze flit from cabin to cabin and then to the pond and from there to the fields of grain and the cattle pastures beyond. She really should have been born to a rancher, he mused. She'd have loved growing up out here, playing in the haymow and swinging on the tree rope with him and his brothers and sisters and cousins. He had to admit, it was an idyllic way to grow up. Still, they'd been far from poor.

But the money hadn't mattered. Hadn't corrupted. Dakota knew the whole family would have been just as happy without a cent to their name.

Dakota filled his lungs with sweet country air and slowly expelled it through tight lips. "It's showtime." He leaned forward and kissed Elizabeth on the mouth. "For luck," he murmured.

"Thanks," she whispered, her voice quivering with excitement. "I'm going to need it."

"Sit tight for a second and I'll come around and help you down."

"Okay."

Dakota jumped to the ground and slammed his door. Catching the eyes of his ranch hands, he signaled them to join him at the back of the truck. Voice low, he gestured everyone into a huddle of sorts.

"Listen up," he commanded. "Did Fuzzy tell you guys what's going on?" At their affirmative nods, he continued. "Great. I'll give five thousand bucks to the guy who does the best acting job and convinces Victoria that Elizabeth and I are really married and have been for a month."

There were some low whistles and delighted expletives.

"Shh." Dakota looked back over his shoulder to see if the coast was clear. Simon was still parking. Good. "Plus,

I'll give an extra grand here and there for best efforts to make Victoria feel just like one of the family." He grinned. "Kill her with countrified kindness. That drives her nuts. With any luck, she'll be headed back to Dallas before sundown tomorrow."

"Gotcha, boss." The hands all nodded.

"Fuzzy, Red, you two will give the ladies a tour of the place in the morning to keep them busy until I can get away for lunch."

Montana scratched the five o'clock shadow at his jaw. "Just so we're all on the same page, here, big brother, you don't want any of us to take her past Big Daddy's main house or the oil rigs, right?"

"Excellent point." Dakota thumbed his Stetson back on his head. "Keep them away from anything that smacks of money. They think we're poor and I want to keep it that way until I can figure out how to break it to Elizabeth gently."

"I gotta say, boss, that's the strangest thing I ever heard of, a woman not liking the finer things in life." Fuzzy scratched his head. "Don't seem natural somehow."

"Yeah. I know what you mean, but it's one of the main reasons I love her."

"Love?" The ranch hands all hooted at that, and jabbed each other in the guts.

"Shut up." Ignoring them, Dakota moved toward Elizabeth's door. "Remember what I said," he mouthed over his shoulder. "Five grand for the best actor."

Onboard with this incentive plan, the guys all moved toward the limousine to begin their job.

Finally, Simon had the limousine snugly in place and was helping Victoria out of the backseat. Nose wrinkled, and fumbling for her oxygen mask, she took several deep, cleansing breaths as she swung her feet to the ground.

Once she'd alighted on the unpaved road, she began picking her way through the cow and horse paddies that littered the area. Simon brought up the rear with the oxygen tank, though it was clear to all that she was merely breathing the bottled air to avoid the smell of ranch life.

There were several horses tied up to an old-fashioned hitching post in front of one of the cabins. Curious, the horses swiveled their heads to watch Victoria's progress, lazily flicking flies off their haunches with their tails. Ears twitching, they listened to her nonstop barrage of complaints, their low nickers sounding almost reproachful in response.

As Victoria wobbled down the road toward her granddaughter, Colt tore off his hat and threw it over a horse paddy. "To save your shoes, ma'am," he said, then bowed.

Not to be outdone, Hunt stripped off his vest and threw it on the ground in front of Colt's hat. "What we don't have in pavement, we make up for in courtesy," he claimed with a grin.

Buttons popping, Sly tore off his shirt and flung it down.

Victoria gasped, not sure whether to be thankful or appalled as she looked at the robust body of the sinewy, tan cowboy.

Dakota approached with Elizabeth and held up a hand to forestall any further stripping. "Nice work men, but I can carry her from here."

"You'll do no such thing," Victoria shouted and clobbered his powerful bicep with her bony fist as he bent to pick her up.

Dakota grinned and took several big steps back. He had to admit, Victoria had spunk. He liked that about her. Reminded him of Elizabeth.

Montana pushed past Colt and Hunt and beating Sly to

the punch, reached for Elizabeth. "Sis!" With a flourish, he bent her over backward and planted a bunch of noisy kisses on her cheeks. "It's so good to have you home, dollface. We've missed you something fierce."

Still dangling backward in his embrace, Elizabeth flushed bright red and, cupping her fiery cheeks in her palms, looked up at him with wide eyes. "Why, er…uh, Montana, you're so sweet. I…why, I've missed you all, too."

Grin wide and still cradling her just above the ground, Montana quirked a mischievous brow at the guys. "Was there ever a more beautiful sister-in-law?" He shook his head and growled down at her, then glanced up at the now frowning Dakota. "When it came to picking a woman, you did good, brother. I always say that, though, don't I?"

"He always says that," Fuzzy agreed. "Twice, sometimes three times a day."

"We all say it," Colt said.

"Sometimes more than three times a day," Sly added.

"Ever since they got married, back there, several…" Red reddened, "…weeks ago back in…uh, back in…" He blanched and mortified, held up several callused fingers and did the math as everyone held a collective breath. "July?"

"Right." Dakota nodded as everyone resumed breathing.

"Yep. They got married in July." Montana swooped Elizabeth back upright and draped a familiar arm around her shoulders. "If you weren't married to my brother, I'd make a play for you myself, Sis." He sighed. "But you're married."

"They're married." Fuzzy nodded in agreement.

Rolling his eyes, Dakota strode over and took Elizabeth by the hand, nudging his brother out of the way. "I said make *Victoria* feel welcome,'' he gritted out between clenched teeth.

"Ohhh.'' Montana nodded as if only just now understanding the rules then winked at Elizabeth. "Anyhow, if I couldn't have ya, the next best thing is you marrying my brother.''

"Yep,'' Red said. "She married Dakota.''

"They're married all right,'' Fuzzy put in.

"Been married for one month,'' Colt added.

Dakota pushed his lips up at the corners to mask his disgust. Maybe offering these clowns money hadn't been such a good idea after all.

Expression sour, Victoria huffed on her oxygen mask and, batting wildly at the flies that buzzed about her head, demanded, "Why in the hell are we just standing around out here? Where's your bunk bed?'' She cast her suspicious gaze at Dakota.

"Right, Nanna, right. We need to get you inside.'' Two long strides carried him back to her side, where he took the arm that Simon wasn't supporting. "By the way, guys, this here is Elizabeth's Nanna.''

"Stop calling me that disgusting name,'' Victoria snapped.

"Nanna, these are the guys. Nanna, here, is a makeup tycoon.''

The men all doffed their hats. "Ma'am. How do,'' they inquired politely.

Victoria sniffed and looked down her nose at them like a queen overlooking her subjects. She dabbed at her melting mascara with a lace hanky, then tore her mask from her face long enough to say, "I'll be doing much better when I get out of this wretched heat. The stench alone is killing me.''

"We can't have that.'' Dakota dug into his pocket for

a dollar bill and locating one, crushed it into Simon's hand. "Here ya go, buddy. Why don't you unload Nanna's bags and bring 'em to the house. Guys, give him a hand."

The hands—with the exception of Fuzzy who sidled up to Victoria—all rushed to comply.

Grizzled face beaming, Fuzzy took Victoria's hand and brought it to his lips for the lightest of kisses. "Elizabeth, I can see where you get your beauty," he called over his shoulder.

"Oh, spare me," Victoria crabbed and batted him away. Then she pecked at Elizabeth's arm with a knobby finger and nodded toward the bunkhouses. "Which one of these monstrosities is your bunk bed?"

"I...uh, it's over..." Elizabeth looked helplessly about.

"Right this way." Dakota propelled Victoria forward and patted Elizabeth on the arm. "Let me help you with your bags, sweetheart. I bet you're glad to be home."

Elizabeth sighed and inadvertently headed toward the wrong cabin. "I'll say."

"*This* way, honey," Dakota said, guiding her with her suitcase.

"Oh, of course." Her giggle was flustered. "I was... just...going...to go check on something."

"Sure you were, honey, but you can do that later." He winked at her. "It's good to have you back home where you belong."

As they headed down the dirt road to the far cabin, she lifted her lashes to him, her eyes shining with what looked to him like genuine happiness. "It's good to be home," she breathed. "Very good."

Simon lost no time in handing Victoria's bags off to the guys, and taking his leave. Before they even made it to Dakota's bunkhouse, great billows of dust swirled out from

under the limousine as he made good his escape down the
road and back to civilization. Watching him depart from
the walkway in front of Dakota's bunkhouse, Elizabeth's
smile was rueful. So. She was stranded here, out in the
middle of nowhere with Victoria for the next week. Hardly
her dream vacation. However, with Dakota at her side,
even a week spent confined with Victoria promised to be
exciting, at the very least. She crossed her fingers for luck.
Surely, this ride would be wilder than any Dakota had ever
experienced before on the rodeo circuit.

With Fuzzy and Red flanking Victoria behind them and
Montana and the others bringing up the rear, Dakota led
Elizabeth up the porch steps to the front door of his home.
For a fleeting moment, she had the absurd notion that she
was coming here as his bride and—as if he could read her
mind—he swept her into his arms. A swift kick to the
screen door with his booted foot had it banging open and
he swept her over the threshold.

Arms looped around his neck, Elizabeth leaned back and
laughed. It was wonderful to be home. Her fantasy had
finally come true. As Dakota gently set her on her feet, she
looked around the cozy interior of the little cabin and felt
a lump begin to swell in her throat.

The guys had outdone themselves to make it look as if
she'd been living there as Dakota's wife. And, though they
were a little haphazard and ignorant of the way a woman
ran a household in the new millennium, it was evident that
their hearts were in the right place.

From the living room, Elizabeth could see several pairs
of panty hose draped over the shower rod. Her cheeks
burned hot as she spied one of her nightgowns slung over
a dining room chair. She glanced at Dakota and he
shrugged, a wide grin splitting his face. Lingerie was scattered hither and yon, as if all their waking hours not spent

at work were spent...making love. Here. There. Every-where.

The guys all stifled grins behind their hands.

Victoria arched a brow, but made no comment as Elizabeth kicked a pile of satin under the couch and invited her to come in and get settled in her room. Whichever room that was. Leading the way, Elizabeth explored the area off the kitchen-dining-living room combo. At the end of a short hallway was the one, and only, bathroom. On either side of that, was a single bedroom. Which one belonged to Dakota was anyone's guess.

Pausing in the bathroom doorway, she peeked quickly inside. Her pink toothbrush was hanging next to Dakota's in the holder. Men's fingers had fiddled with her cosmetics and, to make them look as if someone had been using them, there were lipstick prints on a tissue. Elizabeth was touched by the image of Fuzzy or Red doing something so silly, just for her. She swallowed and with a gentle pressure at her waist from Dakota, headed toward what she presumed was his bedroom.

The men had strewn rose petals on the bed.

"They thought of everything," Dakota mumbled under his breath.

Elizabeth was overcome by the sweetness of their gesture. She cupped Fuzzy's cheek in her hand and gave him a little kiss. "Thank you."

Fuzzy fairly floated off the floor. "No problem."

Victoria, thumping along behind them, demanded, "Where in the devil is my bunk bed? I've had a long, grueling day, and the sooner I can lie down—even if it is in these crude, unsanitary conditions—the better."

"Right this way, Nanna." Dakota carted her luggage to Montana's bedroom and set it down inside the door. "You can rest up in here."

His arm swept the masculine room, simply furnished with bookshelves laden with rodeo trophies and framed fishing pictures of the Brubaker boys and their catches. The wood floors were bare except for a few scatter rugs, and the knotty pine walls sported the taxidermied heads of several wild animals, the most prominent being the moose that was mounted over the bed.

"Go ahead and have a lay down, Nanna," Dakota encouraged. "But don't get too comfy."

"I doubt that will be a concern." Victoria eyed the moose head with disdain.

"Good. Good. Elizabeth is gonna barbecue for all of us this afternoon for an early supper and mark my words, you won't want to miss that."

Elizabeth beamed. "I'll make Ned's special recipe. Hope you all like ribs."

"Love 'em, don't we guys?" Dakota planted his hands on her shoulders and massaged the delicate muscles at her nape and wished that they were alone and on their honeymoon and not in the middle of some complex Shakespearean farce.

Fuzzy and Red smacked their lips in affirmation.

Victoria sank to the edge of the bed.

Dakota turned Elizabeth in his arms and knowing he had Victoria's full attention, nibbled her lower lip. "I'll help you do whatever grocery shopping needs to be done in town after I check in at the office. Then we'll get cookin'."

She leaned against him and snaked her hands up around the back of his neck. "Anyone ever tell you that you're a wonderful husband?" With a sigh, she kissed him, ignoring the hee haws and the hoots from the guys.

After dinner that evening, Elizabeth and Victoria sat together at a picnic table on the small deck situated at the back of Dakota and Montana's bunkhouse. Everyone was chock-full of ribs and corn on the cob and the guys were all playing horseshoes on the lawn and whooping it up before strawberry shortcake and ice cream was served for dessert. The sun had traveled just over the western horizon and a magical twilight was slowly lengthening the shadows. Occasionally, the *tzeet* of an unlucky insect landing in the purple light of the bug zapper or the clink of a horseshoe finding its mark would startle Victoria as she sipped at her tea and harangued Elizabeth to come home and take over the business.

Try as she might to make Victoria understand, it was futile and Elizabeth finally tuned her out and focused on the horseshoe match.

The ribs had been an unmitigated success and, though Victoria pretended scorn, it escaped no one's attention that she'd had a second helping. After dinner, the dishes had all been cleared, washed and put away in a fashion that had Elizabeth delirious with the hilarity of it all. Men were stumbling over themselves to welcome Victoria to the family and convince her that Elizabeth's marriage was not only real, it was flourishing. And, though they'd made every effort to include and be kind to Victoria, the elder woman observed the good-natured shenanigans with a persnickety pucker between her brows. A happy-go-lucky household was foreign to her experience and Elizabeth could tell she was masking her confusion with ill temper.

When Dakota made yet another ringer and flexed his muscles for his bride, she clapped and catcalled in an unladylike fashion that had Victoria shaking her head. Elizabeth didn't care. With the exception of her grandmother's incessant nagging, she was having the time of her life. It was so easy to imagine that she was fulfilling all of her childhood dreams that evening. The joyful, uncomplicated lifestyle was hers, as well as the cabin, the simple furnishings, and…the man. Easy banter from the men underscored this daydream.

"Hooboy, Dakota," Fuzzy yelled as his boss missed striking the post by an inch or two. "You can do better than that. Married life has made you soft, son."

"Hey. I resemble that remark," Dakota said, affably.

"Ever since he married Elizabeth, a month or so ago, back there in July, he's gone to pot," Red put in.

"Hear tell a month or two of marriage is all it takes for the honeymoon to be over. That true, Dakota?" Clay wondered.

Dakota snorted and cast a roguish glance in Elizabeth's direction. "No."

Elizabeth peeped at Victoria to see if she was buying all this talk about her marriage. It seemed to her that they might be laying it on just a tad thick. Even so, who was she to complain? It was simply amazing how eager these sweet men were to help her out. They must really enjoy working for Dakota, to go out of their way, so selflessly. And could she blame them?

He was a wonderful man.

Finally, the tournament came to an end and the guys trundled back up to the deck for some shortcake.

His plate heaped with dessert, Montana stabbed a strawberry with his fork and looked with mischief at Elizabeth. "You know, Sis, I gotta tell you I love what you've done with the place. It's not the same at all, since you moved in."

Elizabeth blushed furiously, knowing that he was referring to the lingerie that had pretty much carpeted the floor.

Dakota chuckled. "Me, too. I'm telling you guys, before Elizabeth moved in, the place had no sense of style."

"No romance," Red put in.

Fuzzy nodded, his cheeks turning to whiskered apples with his grin. "No *joie de vivre*."

"Oh," she said demurely, "well, I only wish I'd had time to straighten up, before we left to go to Dallas for the weekend. Normally, I don't leave my…er…delicates in such a mess."

The hands all slapped their thighs and laughed around mouths full of shortcake and ice cream. Victoria stared at them.

Soon, the dessert was polished off and a challenge was issued for one last do-or-die round of horseshoes. The men thundered off the deck and onto the grass, leaving Elizabeth alone once more with Victoria.

"Having a good time, Grandmother?"

Victoria harrumphed. "This bench is harder than a rock and the mosquitoes are eating me alive. It's hot out here." She dabbed her ruby red lips with a napkin. "And this little hovel is a disgrace. How can you claim to be happy? If you would just come home with me, you could have everything."

"Can't you see, Grandmother? I have everything right here. I feel like the richest woman on the face of this earth, when Dakota smiles at me." There was an unmistakable truth in her tone that she knew Victoria couldn't miss.

As if he felt her stare, Dakota looked through the twilight, to smile at her. Through the soft shadows, he blew her a kiss, then turned and tossed the horseshoe. It was a perfect ringer. A cry of jubilation arose from the guys.

Reaching across the table, Elizabeth clasped Victoria's hand in her own and gently rubbed the paper-thin skin with the pad of her thumb. "Grandmother," she paused, and, groping for the proper words, tried to quell the emotion that rose in her throat, "Dakota makes me happier than

I've ever been before. It's a feeling I could never buy. Not with any amount of money.''

And somehow, Elizabeth thought fleetingly, she had to keep her family from scaring him off. Just as soon as Victoria was on her way home and she was no longer obligated to him, she would confess her true feelings and hope that, even though he claimed he wasn't ready for a relationship, he'd make an exception for her.

Elizabeth's gaze flitted to Victoria's face. For the briefest of moments, she thought she saw melancholy mixed with envy flash in her eyes.

But that couldn't be.

''Where are you going?'' Her voice barely above a whisper, Elizabeth tiptoed into Dakota's bedroom from the bathroom.

It was nearly midnight and Victoria had been tucked away an hour ago. Despite the older lady's claims that the moose head would cause incurable insomnia, her hearty snores could be heard from behind her bedroom door.

Fresh from the shower, Elizabeth was wearing a terry cloth robe. A bath towel was wrapped turban style over her damp head. Even devoid of a speck of makeup and wearing his old robe that fit her like a gunny sack, she was breathtaking. Long, shapely legs peeked from beneath the robe and her toenails were painted a dusty shade of rose.

''I have some work to catch up on down at the office.''

Dakota reached to his dresser for the keys to the office. He had to get out of there. Staying all night with her in such close proximity was dangerous. She wasn't ready for this. And he was. It was as simple, and as complicated, as that.

She glanced at the clock on his nightstand. ''At this hour?''

"Ranch don't quit runnin' on weekends." His excuse was thin, and he suspected she knew it.

"Oh. Right." Tugging the towel from her head, she began to dry the ends of her hair. "How long are you going to be gone?"

"Couple of hours at the least. Got some papers to shuffle…"

"Ah." She sank to the edge of the mattress and looked up at him with a grateful smile. "I hope you don't mind that I borrowed your robe. The guys didn't pack me much in the way of substantial nightclothes and I left my other robe at Victoria's…" Her voice trailed off, and she cast a bashful glance at the floor.

"No. That's fine."

"Thanks. Oh, and before you go, I just want to thank you for letting me come here today, with Grandmother. The guys were so sweet with her and even though she's too cranky to admit it, I think she had an old-fashioned good time."

"I'm glad." He moved to the end of the bed and leaned against the footboard. He longed to take the towel from her hands and run it over her head, drying her hair and feeling the silky softness of the strands.

"You know, I think she might just be starting to think it's hopeless." She looked up at him from under the heavy fringe of her lashes.

"What's hopeless?"

Bashfully, she said, "Well, I think she is really beginning to get the feeling that we are in love."

His pulse crested the hill it had been thundering up and began to chug down, picking up speed, roaring in his ears. He bit his lower lip and willed the brakes to slow his runaway heart. "What's tipping her off?"

The color in her cheeks heightened. "I think we can give

some of the credit to your ability as an actor.'' She waved her hand around. ''You know, for pretending to be crazy about me.''

It's no act, Dakota wanted to shout. He felt a sudden urgency to come clean with her. To tell her the truth about his financial situation. To tell her how much she meant to him. To tell her that he was in love with her and that he would sacrifice anything and everything, just to be with her.

But right here and right now, all he could think of was how beautiful she looked.

He needed time to think.

He needed to get out of there.

He needed to figure out a way to make her understand that, though the love of money was the root of all evil, money itself wasn't. They could still live her fantasy life, without having to renounce their families and everything they'd worked so hard to achieve.

Tomorrow. He would talk to her tomorrow.

He would tell her he loved her first.

And then, when they were alone and the time was right, he'd tell her about his own family's fortune.

With a long, slow exhalation, Dakota looked into her face, so guileless and soft in the lamplight. Telling her the news was going to be tricky. She'd been so hurt by the greed in her own family.

He flexed his hands. ''You know, someday, you may fall in love with a man who has a lot of money. And, you might just find happiness.''

Elizabeth blinked, trying to disguise the hurt that suddenly brimmed in her eyes. ''Impossible.'' The whispered word was barely audible.

For a long, tension filled moment, he stared at her with a yearning so strong, it robbed him of his breath. Then, against his better judgment, he leaned ever so slowly over the end of the bed and cupping her chin in his palm, drew her mouth beneath his. He kissed her with an urgency that even he hadn't realized raged within. Dropping the towel in her lap, her hands came up and she clutched his shoulders and returned his kiss with all the passion he felt pent up in his own soul.

Mouths hungry, breathing labored, hands searching, probing the contours of each other's faces, jawlines, throats, they melded together, moving as one being.

Elizabeth strained toward him, moving her hands to the back of his neck, threading her fingers in his hair. Dakota leaned over the end of the bed and battled the temptation to climb over the footboard and join her.

But he couldn't.

Not until she knew the truth about her pseudo-husband.

Not until he was her husband.

Tearing his mouth from hers, he stood up and took a step back. He dragged a hand through his hair and let his gaze flit around the room. If he looked at her again, he'd be lost.

"I gotta go."

Elizabeth nodded, mute.

"I'll be back. Later."

After he'd sorted this mess out in his mind.

After she was sound asleep. Long after.

Chapter Ten

The first tentative rays of dawn were just peeking through the windows the next morning, when Elizabeth heard the front door of Dakota's bunkhouse open. Emerging from the bedroom, she tugged at the sash of his old robe and moved down the short hall to peek into the living room.

Dakota was finally home.

He'd been gone all night long. She knew this because she'd been awake until the wee hours, waiting for him to return. Finally, just before the sun came up, she drifted into a fitful slumber. But it didn't last.

Her heart turned over and guilt suddenly flared in her belly. He looked shredded. No doubt he'd spent the better part of the night working to make up for the time he'd missed over the weekend helping her in Dallas.

"Good morning," she whispered.

As he softly closed the door, he looked up, the little lines at the corners of his shadowed eyes bunched. "Morning."

"How are you?"

"Fine, now that I see you."

A slow heat crawled up her neck. Always the perfect gentleman. "Did you get any sleep?"

He shrugged. "A little."

He'd probably been slaving away in an uncomfortable desk chair while she kept him from his bed. Feeling awkward under his piercing gaze, she gestured toward the kitchen. "Want some breakfast? I could put on some coffee."

"No. Thanks. I really need to talk to you."

"Okay." Elizabeth swallowed.

Something about the inflection in his tone made her nervous. She braced herself for the inevitable. Had they finally come to the end of his patience with this whole charade? She wouldn't blame him. She'd taken huge advantage of his good nature, and he'd been wonderful. But now, here she was, invading his territory. And he had work to do. It was time to go. She would go pack now. Victoria would be thrilled when she announced that they were going home.

Her lips quivered as she returned his smile. "What, uh, do you need to talk to me about?"

"Well, I need to tell you a few important things. Later. When we have a few minutes alone. Away from," he gestured back toward Victoria's bedroom, "everyone."

Elizabeth nodded, her gaze darting to the wide, knotty pine plank flooring. "Okay."

As if sensing her discomfort, he crossed the room and clasped her hands in his. "But, first, I have to tell you one thing, and it can't wait."

She tried to swallow, but the muscles in her throat seized, making it impossible. "Uh-huh."

Dakota drew her hands up and cradled them against his heart. His gaze sought hers, probing, searching for what, she didn't know. "Elizabeth," he paused and closed his eyes, "all night long I debated whether or not I should tell you this now. But, given the nature of our relationship, I knew I just couldn't wait any longer.''

Oh, no. Her heart pounded. Her stomach churned. *Given the nature of our relationship.* What did that mean? Something intimate in his gaze made her know that he could see into her heart. He was onto her. He knew she was falling in love with him and the feeling was not mutual. A high pitched whine buzzed in her ears and she felt faint. *Just say it,* she wanted to scream. Get it over with. ''Yes?'' she whispered.

''Elizabeth, I'm afraid,'' he touched his tongue to his lips and she was sure her heart failed, ''I'm afraid I've fallen in love with you.''

She could see his lips moving, but the words didn't penetrate. That he didn't love her was obvious, however, by the tortured look on his face. ''Oh.''

''I have been in love with you ever since I laid eyes on you, your first day on the job down at Ned's place.''

What?

The buzzing began to ebb. Did he just say what she thought he said? She stared up at his lips, willing herself to understand.

''I know,'' he said, taking a deep breath, ''that you are not looking for a relationship, especially since that disaster with Bernard and I respect that—''

''No,'' she breathed, clutching his hands. ''No!'' That wasn't true at all. She would *love* a relationship with him.

''Right. I understand.'' He exhaled, his smile self-deprecating and melancholy. ''I can see I've made you uncomfortable. I'm really sorry to lay this on you. It's just that I couldn't wait another second to tell you the truth. At least that much of it.'' He traced the contours of her knuckles with his fingertips and sighed. ''I'm so sorry—''

"No!" Elizabeth interrupted as joy replaced the dread in her heart.

"No?"

"No. Don't be sorry." Elizabeth's heart took wing as she gazed into his eyes. "I love you, too."

As the reality of her words sank in, his face was transformed with elation. "You do?"

"I do."

For the longest moment, he simply stared at her, digesting this revelation, until a slow, lazy smile pushed his dimples into being. The heart that had failed her only moments before began to race. A possessive look that had her stomach tingling, flashed in his eyes.

With a groan, he let go of her hands and threading his fingers into the hair at the nape of her neck, stroked her jaw with his thumbs.

"Oh, Elizabeth," he said softly. Heat coursed through her body as he settled his mouth over hers and kissed her with all the passion she suspected he'd held in check before. Rapidly, the kiss grew urgent. Heated. His breathing was labored as he backed her up against the living room wall and deepened the kiss.

Volts of electricity shot down her spine and, in Elizabeth's mind, time stood still.

A shaft of sunlight streamed through the window, bathing them in its warm, magical morning twilight. Outside, birdsong wafted on the gentle breezes and the lowing of cattle could be heard off in the distance. Intoxicated by the unbearable sweetness of knowing that Dakota loved her, dazed thoughts flitted through her mind. This was paradise. No amount of money could ever buy the joy she felt at this moment. Poor Victoria. How could she have thrown away a life of happiness and love to run a cold and unfeeling company?

Dakota released her lips just long enough to groan, "I don't wanna go to work today."

Elizabeth sighed, her breath mingling with his. "I don't want you to."

"I could call in sick and we could elope."

Giddy mirth bubbled into her throat. She knew he was teasing, but the idea was immensely appealing. "What would we do with Grandmother?"

"Hasn't she given up on you yet?"

"She's tenacious."

Dakota sighed. "So am I. I'm serious about eloping." Propping himself on his elbows against the wall, he leaned into her body. "Would you consider marrying me?"

"Yes. But…" She gazed up at him, feeling suddenly in awe of this wonderful man. This man who knew her family history, yet still wanted her. "You'd marry someone who was foolish enough to walk away from a fortune?"

"I don't care about money, if you don't."

"You know I don't."

"Good. I'm going to hold you to that."

"Mmm. Just hold *me*."

He slid one arm around her waist and spoke between the kisses he rained along the edge of her jaw. "I still have a few things I need to discuss with you, but," he nodded toward Victoria's room where they could hear her stirring, "that will have to wait until later. Why don't you and I go for a long walk after dinner tonight?"

Elizabeth smiled. "Sounds heavenly."

"Then it's a date."

"It's a date."

Lost in the sweet bliss of their newfound mutual love, they didn't realize that they were no longer alone. Sleep mask perched atop her spongy pink curlers, Victoria emerged from her room and stared at them.

"Don't the two of you ever get tired of pawing at each other?"

"Good morning, Nanna," Dakota murmured, never taking his eyes from Elizabeth.

With a sigh, Victoria shuffled into the bathroom. Before she threw the door shut she called back in a resigned tone, "Stop calling me that disgusting name."

She'd dressed while Dakota had taken a shower. Her head still reeling, and her heart soaring with happiness, Elizabeth managed to get breakfast on the table. Dakota helped, when he wasn't waylaying her with some transparent excuse or other to kiss her, or touch her in passing. The toast was burned, the cereal was soggy and the eggs were tough, but only Victoria seemed to care.

When Victoria wasn't complaining about the accommodations, she was grousing about their sickening behavior, claiming it was enough to rot her dentures. Luckily, just as she was getting cranked up, Fuzzy and Red arrived to escort her and Elizabeth on a tour of the ranch. Hats in hand, they nodded and called a friendly greeting to Victoria who harrumphed into her mug.

"Are you ladies ready?" Fuzzy enquired.

Victoria grabbed her cane and thump-hitched past him to the front door. "I don't suppose I have any choice. Although, I guess anything is better than sitting here watching these two carry on."

Elizabeth snagged her sunglasses from her purse and spent a moment kissing Dakota goodbye. "I'll see you back here at noon for lunch?"

"Can't wait." Reluctantly, Dakota released her to Fuzzy's care.

"We know you have seen the whole place a hundred times, Elizabeth," Fuzzy said for Victoria's benefit as he escorted her to the front door, ''but we thought you'd enjoy spending some time with your Nanna.''

''Stop calling me that,'' Victoria's voice wafted to them from the porch.

Smiling at the old girl's curmudgeonly tone, Dakota detained Red. ''Just be sure that you don't accidentally drive them past any of the oil fields, or the main house.''

''No problem,'' Red assured him. ''We got the route all mapped out. We should have 'em back here just before noon, and Nanna there, should just about be ready to head back to Dallas by then.''

''Where are you taking them?''

''Pretty much in circles. Might stop and show off some of the cattle here and there, but mostly, we'll be circling sections seven through twelve.''

''Go easy out there in section eight. That's pretty bumpy. Don't want to give Nanna whiplash.''

''Right, boss.''

Dakota watched out the window as Fuzzy settled the women into Big Daddy's ranch jeep.

Elizabeth loved him. He still couldn't quite believe his luck. Now, all he had to do was tell her the rest of the story and they could begin living happily ever after. He hoped.

''Well, that was horrific,'' Victoria crabbed as she slowly settled her tiny frame into a chair on Dakota's front porch after having spent a grueling morning touring thousands of acres in a dusty jeep. Pulling a compact from her pocket, she flipped it open and, inspecting her appearance in the mirror, dabbed some powder on her dirt-speckled nose and cheeks. ''Those two rubes are certifiably nuts.''

Victoria was referring to Fuzzy and Red who'd just

dropped them off after speeding back to the ranch offices to answer an emergency page from Dakota. Apparently a prize bull had broken out of his pen and was on the loose. All available hands were needed to round up this mean-tempered—and hugely valuable—critter.

"All I can say is thank God for that bull," Victoria groused, "or we'd still be out there, exploring the infinitely wonderful world of Buffalo Prairie versus Coastal Bermuda grass." Once she'd freshened her lipstick and spritzed on some cologne, she peered from beneath her false eyelashes at Elizabeth. "What's next? Chinese water torture?"

Elizabeth grinned as she moved up to the porch railing and perched opposite her grandmother. "Nothing that drastic. As soon as Dakota comes home after rounding up that bull, we're going to take you to lunch at Ned's for a Longhorn burger."

Victoria snorted. "Dare I dream?"

"Come on, Grandmother. It'll be fun. You said you wanted to find out what I enjoy so much about being poor."

"And, I'm still waiting. Surely you can't be serious about giving up Lindon House for this."

"I am. More than ever."

Before Victoria could begin haranguing in earnest, the front door of the ranch office banged open, drawing their attention. A diminutive elf of a man in a ten-gallon hat emerged and trotted down the gravel road, heading toward the luxurious Land Rover that was parked in front of Dakota's bunkhouse. As the man approached, he noticed Elizabeth and Victoria sitting on Dakota's porch and a wide grin of greeting transformed his rubbery face.

"Why, how do, ladies!"

Flustered, Elizabeth returned his wave and glanced at

Victoria. She couldn't be sure, but from Dakota's description she guessed that his must be his uncle Big Daddy. "Fine, thanks," she called gaily, and hoped he would hop into his Land Rover and be on his way.

No such luck.

He jogged from the road to the walkway and bounded right up the front steps and onto the porch.

"Gonna be a scorcher today," he cried and taking off his hat, mopped his brow with a handkerchief the size of a small tablecloth. "You lovely ladies shouldn't be sittin' out here in this heat. Why it's enough to melt a couple of delicate flowers such as yourselves." His tiny boots clomped across the floorboards to Victoria and he extended his hand. "I'm Big Daddy Brubaker, and you must be," his raisin-like gaze flitted to Elizabeth and he raised a curious brow, "Elizabeth's grandmother?"

"Yes." Victoria stared down her nose and nodded.

"Well now, isn't that dandy?" Big Daddy patted her hand then turned to face Elizabeth. "Howdy, sweetheart. Good to see ya."

"Hello, Big Daddy. It's good to see you, too." Elizabeth relaxed. Dakota must have filled his uncle in on what was going on with Victoria. She looked into his kindly face and was immediately and inexplicably drawn to him. Must run in the family, she mused. "We just returned from giving Grandmother a tour of your ranch," she explained, returning his exuberant hug.

"Isn't it beautiful?" Big Daddy cried.

Victoria snorted.

"I think so, too," Big Daddy agreed, mistaking her response for awe. "So, what are you two ladies doin' sittin' out here all alone?"

"Waiting for Dakota. He's going to take us to Hidden Valley for lunch as soon as he gets home."

"Ah. That's nice. Well, lambchop, he's gonna be a while. Heard some of the hands talkin' over the radio just now 'bout that bull and it 'pears he's headed for the border." Big Daddy's laughter boomed. "Why don't you both come with me up to the house? I've got a pitcher of lemonade with your name on it," he tempted.

Elizabeth vacillated. Dakota was expecting to meet them here. However, she supposed if she left him a note, he'd know where to find her. And besides, Big Daddy was delightful. Obviously in on the ruse, he was playing his part of gracious in-law to perfection.

"All right," she agreed, looking to Victoria for any sign of refusal. For once, there was none. "Lemonade sounds wonderful."

As Dakota bounded up the front steps to his bunkhouse, his excitement at coming home to Elizabeth faded and a feeling of unexplainable dread filled his gut. Things were quiet. Too quiet. He pulled open the screen door and a small sheet of paper fluttered to the floor.

The brief note was scrawled in Elizabeth's hand.

Hi, honey,
Big Daddy stopped by and invited us up to his place for some lemonade.
Why don't you meet us there before we head to Ned's?

Love,
Elizabeth

An innocent row of *x's* and *o's* decorated the edge of the missive.

Dakota's entire life flashed before his eyes.

They must be up at the mansion.

And Big Daddy was the one guy he hadn't clued in about Elizabeth's aversion to money. Boots airborne, he was back down the steps in one giant leap and a second later, gunning the engine to his truck. He shoved the truck into gear and, tires spinning, gravel flying, headed down the road toward the Circle BO mansion.

"All my sons and nephews run the ranch for a while before they step up to the plate at Brubaker International. By this time next year, as Dakota has no doubt told you—" Big Daddy was boasting to his captive audience of two "—he will be taking his place on the family board. He'll also take ovah as CEO of two of his daddy's Fortune 1000 holdings."

Completely dumbfounded, Elizabeth allowed her gaze to travel the room where she and Victoria were being served lemonade in frosty crystal goblets. The book-lined baronial library, with its lush velvet draperies and polished brass andirons was, if possible, even more elegant and tastefully decorated than Victoria's. And the house—a huge antebellum mansion—was breathtaking.

A short time ago, as Big Daddy had turned the Land Rover onto his impressive, tree-lined drive, Elizabeth had to wonder at first if he was speaking figuratively when he referred to the house as 'his place.' Perhaps all of the hired help felt this way about their place of employment? Surely, he couldn't *own* this place.

Pillars, like sturdy sentinels, guarded the house proper, supporting what looked to Elizabeth like acres of verandah on the first and second floors. The fantastic surrounding area was dotted with more then a half dozen other charming buildings, including the servants quarters, a giant garage, the poolhouse, a gazebo, a greenhouse and a number of stables. Big Daddy had led them to the library through an enormous foyer, shouting orders to a servant as he went for lemonade to be delivered posthaste.

How could this be?

As she sat listening to Big Daddy fill Victoria in on his family's history, lightbulbs began to click on ever so slowly in Elizabeth's mind. A sheen of perspiration dotted her suddenly feverish brow and, at the same time, icy gooseflesh crawled up her spine and spread to her limbs. She battled nausea and struggled to remain conscious.

It was happening again.

That cursed Midas touch. Once again, it was all turning to gold.

Beside her, she noticed that Victoria was too stunned by this turn of events to comment.

Dully, Elizabeth turned her gaze to Big Daddy, whose feet dangled boyishly from one of the wine-colored leather wingback chairs in their cozy grouping. It was obvious that he was in no hurry. He seemed to be genuinely glad for their company as he pointed out a number of pictures on the wall where he, and his brother, Tiny, were featured on the covers of *Newsweek* and *Time*.

"That framed article up there pretty much explains our family's history in the oil bidness."

As woodenly as a marionette, Elizabeth stood and wobbled over to the wall. Head swimming, she began to scan the stories, taking in the pictures of the nine Brubaker offspring in each family as Big Daddy continued to chat.

"I gotta tell you both, all my brothers and sisters owe everything we are today, to my mama. Taught us a work ethic that has carried us straight to the top." His good-natured chuckle rumbled around the room. "That's why I like to make all the boys in this family work like dogs before I hand 'em an empire. Makes men out of 'em."

With her back to the door, Elizabeth sensed Dakota's

presence before she could see him. As if by magnetic pull, she turned and their gazes collided.

His expression of guilt said it all.

Hadn't he, only just this morning, said her loved her? How could this be happening? Big Daddy's drone and her own hammering pulse became a blurry roar in her ears. She could feel the blood draining from her face and a lump of betrayal settled like a bolder in the pit of her stomach.

"Why, heah's the man of the hour now." Big Daddy beckoned Dakota in from the hall with a wave of his arm. "Come on in and join us, boy. I was just tellin' Elizabeth's grandmother a little bit about the family."

"I can see that." Dakota cleared his throat and moved into the room and over to where Elizabeth stood near Big Daddy's wall of fame.

"Is it true?" Her voice barely above a whisper, Elizabeth pleaded him with her eyes to say it wasn't so. "Circle BO stands for Brubaker Oil?"

He nodded. "Yes."

"You," she swallowed, blinking back the tears. "You're not who I thought you were at all."

"I wanted to tell you."

She drew herself up and smiled bravely, but she could feel her lower lip tremble as she spoke. "Well, then I guess it's a good thing that our marriage is not real."

Big Daddy's jaw dropped. "Marriage? When did you have time to go and get *married?*"

Victoria's eyes narrowed and she jumped to her feet. With an agility that belied her claims of terminal illness, she rushed, sans cane, to stand beside her granddaughter. "I thought so! You *were* trying to trick me!"

"Victoria, shouldn't you be in bed, what with your *failing* health and all? This excitement can't be good for you." Dakota's tone was sardonic.

"Touché." A spark of admiration flashed in Victoria's eyes and she began to laugh. "So. You are rich. Oh, that is…well, that is rich."

Leaning against the wall, Dakota dragged a hand through his hair. "Yes, ma'am." He sighed heavily. "I guess you could say I'm rich."

"Call me Nanna," she ordered.

The tears that Elizabeth had managed to blink back finally spilled over her lower lashes and cascaded down her cheeks. From the carved cherry-wood end table, she retrieved her purse, slung the strap over her shoulder and brushed past Dakota on her way to the door. "I've got to get out of here."

"Elizabeth wait. I can explain everything."

But Elizabeth was in no mood to be detained.

"Hold on there, boy," Big Daddy called, as Dakota started after her. "What's goin' on? What have you done to make that little gal cry?"

Dakota paused in the doorway, groping for words.

Moving to his side, Victoria waved him off. "You go after your love. I can explain everything to your uncle."

Dakota looked Victoria in the eye. "I'm going to tell her that I'll give it all up for her. And, I'll support her in refusing her inheritance."

Victoria sighed. "Do what you must."

"Nanna," Dakota bent and kissed her rouged cheek, "you are one classy dame."

Victoria smiled. "I know. Go." She patted his arm. "Go."

As Elizabeth marched down the mile long tree-lined driveway, she wished that she had one of Big Daddy's industrial strength handkerchiefs to stem the tidal wave of grief that cascaded down her face. That, and a pair of tennis shoes would be nice. Walking to Hidden Valley in these sandals was going to be hell. But she would do it.

A wretched sob hiccuped past her lips and she swiped at her tears with her fingers. He was rich. His whole blasted family was, by the look of it. Even more disgustingly, filthy rich than her own miserable family.

"Elizabeth."

She could hear Dakota calling her name from somewhere behind her and without looking back, she began to run.

"Elizabeth, stop!"

Ignoring him, she focused on the main road down at the end of the driveway. If she was lucky, she could hitch to town, because she certainly had no intention of listening to him. What possible good could it do? She had no desire to live a pointless life of leisure, when there was so much suffering and homelessness in the world.

A depressing future without Dakota loomed in her mind's eye and she stumbled as a fresh surge of tears blurred her vision.

Breathing heavily from his exertion, Dakota caught her arm and spun her around and pulled her into his embrace.

"Let me go," Elizabeth cried and struggled to pull away.

"No. Not until you hear me out."

Sensing it was futile to try to escape, Elizabeth sagged against him. "I can't believe it. You actually own all of this?"

He sighed and, rocking her back and forth, stroked her hair. "Well, actually, no. My family owns all of this. I just control a portion of it."

"How big a portion? I suppose you're some kind of multimillionaire. You probably have more money than Victoria." Rearing back, she looked up at him and the expression on his face told her everything she needed to know.

"Well, that would depend if you are talking about me personally, or my family as a conglomerate."

"Why didn't you tell me?"

"How could I, when you hate money so much?"

Fresh tears welled into her eyes. "See how hurtful having money can be? See how it destroys?"

"No," Dakota cupped her face in his hands and forced her to look him in the eye, "money has not hurt us. I hurt us by not being honest with you from the beginning." He stroked her cheeks with the rough pads of his fingertips, and there was no mistaking the earnestness behind his words, "But, if it will make you happy, I'll give it all up for you."

"What?" Nonplused, Elizabeth stared. "You would do that? For me?"

"In a heartbeat."

Elizabeth began to cry all over again.

Dakota smiled. "If it will make you happy, we can move into your trailer together and raise that passel of kids we've been talking about. You can work at Ned's and I...well, I'm probably overqualified for just about everything, but I'm sure we can work something out with Big Daddy."

Elizabeth searched his face with her eyes, basking in the light of love that glowed in his eyes. No one had ever offered to do anything so sweet and selfless for her before in her life.

"Honey, I know you've been hurt by your family. I've seen firsthand what you've had to put up with, and I admire you more than I can say. But," he cupped her cheeks with his hands, "I have to tell you, it's not the money that corrupts a family, it's what the family does with it that counts. My clan holds love and family far above money.

I'm sure any one of us would be glad to give up everything for anyone in our family. At any time. Because we're not about money.''

"How can that be?''

"Big Daddy and my father instilled old-fashioned values and the fear of God,'' Dakota chuckled, "in all of us. You know, Elizabeth, I think you should take your Grandmother up on her job offer.''

"What?''

"Well, that way, you could make sure that the money goes to good causes. I've heard you talk about volunteering in the Hidden Valley Soup Kitchen. Why not start there?''

Elizabeth looked at him, silently pondering his words, deeply touched by his thoughtfulness and self-sacrifice. She sniffed and swiped at the tears that would simply not stop.

"I don't deserve you.''

"No,'' Dakota whispered, kissing her tearstained cheeks. "That's my line.''

In spite of her shuddered breathing and tears, Elizabeth pulled back and giggled. "I love you, Dakota Brubaker. In spite of the fact that you are rich.''

"That is probably the nicest thing anyone has ever said to me.'' Dakota grinned his signature grin that had his dimples bracketing his mouth. "Does this mean you'll marry me? For richer or poorer?''

"Mmm.'' Eyes shining, Elizabeth nodded. "Preferably poorer. But,'' she paused and laughed, "with my track record, I wouldn't count on that.''

Epilogue

November, one year later.

"Nanna. There you are." Dakota crossed the industrial style kitchen and took a seat at a massive, old wooden table between Victoria and his wife. Groaning audibly, he leaned back in his chair and, crossing his feet at his ankles, arched back and stretched. Elizabeth reached up and began to rub the muscles at the back of his neck.

"What do you need, honey?" Victoria looked over at him and smiled.

"Simon called." Dakota yawned. "He's coming to pick you up in about an hour."

"So soon?" Victoria sighed. "But it seems like I just got here."

"Time flies, when you're helping the less fortunate." Elizabeth smiled.

"It was a good day." A poignant look crossed Victoria's face as she regarded her granddaughter. "This place," her arm swept the interior of the warehouse that they owned in the heart of Hidden Valley, "is simply amazing. Who'd ever have thought that we could serve Thanksgiving dinner to nearly five hundred underprivileged and homeless in one day? It was remarkable. I'm so proud of you.''

"Me?'' Elizabeth shook her head. "I haven't done all that much. The Lindon House Soup Kitchen was your idea. Mama would have been proud.''

"Well, I don't know.'' Victoria wriggled and shrugged, but it was clear the thought pleased her. "In any event,'' she looked fondly back and forth between Elizabeth and Dakota, "you two handle it like pros. I don't know how you do it, both being so busy running your corporations. And now,'' her expression was soft as she reached past Dakota and patted Elizabeth's swollen middle, "with a baby due at Christmastime.''

"Well, I have to admit, Uncle Ashby and Rainbow and Charles are all a lot of help. We couldn't do it without them.''

"True. Who'd ever have thought? I guess they simply needed a challenge. You know, I don't think there has been a single argument around the dinner table since I put them all to work.''

Dakota laughed. "They're too tired.''

"Well good. I have to admit, I'm pretty pooped myself.''

He frowned. "We didn't work you too hard today, did we?''

"Oh, pshaw. Don't go and treat me like I'm dying.'' There was a twinkle in her eye.

Elizabeth looked at Dakota in amusement. "Now, where would we go and get an idea like that?''

Dakota shrugged. "All I know is, you're too mean to die, Victoria. And that's exactly why I love you.''

Blushing madly, Victoria gathered them close and kissed their cheeks.

* * * * *

*Turn the page for a sneak peek
of the next wonderful installment in
Carolyn Zane's series,*

THE BRUBAKER BRIDES.

Watch for

MONTANA'S FEISTY COWGIRL

*on sale in December,
only from Silhouette Romance.*

Chapter One

Sydney MacKenzie gripped the hem of her skirt and, shifting her hips to-and-fro on the couch, tugged it more firmly down around her knees. Averting her eyes, she feigned rabid fascination with the multicolored pattern in the carpet and tried to appear as if she didn't notice the fact that all eyes in the waiting room to the Circle BO Ranch offices were roving the curves of her legs.

When her head began to swim from staring at the carpet, she—for the dozenth time in less than an hour—rechecked the contents of the manila folder that lay in her lap. Just as it had been only moments ago, everything was still in order. Her resume was impressive and professional, as were the letters of recommendation, references and copies of awards, certificates and degrees.

If paper was anything to go by, she had a good chance at the job. If the competition was any indication—she noted the staring, slobbering faction in her peripheral vision—she already had the job and could start today. Certainly, she had nothing to fear from these sorry excuses for job applicants.

Though she knew it by heart, Sydney's gaze moved over the advertisement she'd torn from the Sunday classifieds.

Wanted:
RANCH HAND/FOREMAN ASSIST. Full-time, perm. Exper. w/wrkng cattle ranch, & some lrg animal med. Ed in Ranch Mgmt a real plus. No stdnts for sumr job, pls. Must be 18. Exclnt wage, bnfts & hsing. Apply: Circle BO Ranch Offices, Hidden Valley, TX.

This certainly described her to a tee. Again, she glanced around and wondered about the qualifications of the other applicants in the room. Woman or not, surely she was the best candidate for the job. She had to be.

Startled back to the moment by the sound of the door to the inner office opening, Sydney tensed as a man's voice called her name.

"MacKenzie?"

She could feel all eyes on her as she stood, gathered her materials and strode purposefully across the room.

"That's me."

She held out her hand and it was enveloped in a strong grip. She was vaguely aware that the man who greeted her was devastatingly handsome, with his dark shock of hair falling rakishly over his forehead and eyes so deep blue that a girl could get the bends if she stared too long. Just her luck. It would have been far easier if he'd been ugly. She disentangled her hand from his and took a slow breath to soothe her jangled nerves.

"I'm Montana Brubaker. Nice to meet you—" there

was a note of surprise in his voice as he checked his clip-board, then allowed his gaze to travel back to her "—*Ms.* MacKenzie." Just behind his friendly dimples, there was the tiniest hint of irritation and impatience in his expression.

Sydney had seen this look before. Obviously, he wasn't expecting a woman. Didn't think she could do the job. She rotated her shoulders. Minor obstacle. Soon, she would have him eating out of the palm of her hand. She flashed him a thousand-watt smile. "Thank you. Please. Call me Sydney."

"Cindy. Okay. Great. Come on in."

"I, uh, it's Syd..." she brushed past him into the cool, ultra-chic interior of his office, "...ney."

"Cindy, this is my uncle, Big Daddy Brubaker."

"Well, howdy theyah," a deep voice boomed, as the swivel chair behind the huge mahogany desk spun around, revealing a diminutive man in a ten-gallon hat that appeared to have swallowed his head. "Pleased to meet up with ya...Cindy." Big Daddy leapt out of his chair to enthusiastically attack Sydney's hand.

"Sydney." She smiled, hoping to smooth the name correction.

"Cindy."

"Sy*d*ney."

"Right. First names are preferable to me, too. So, Cindy. Good. Have a seat."

Okay. No use belaboring the point. The pronunciation of her name was not at issue here. Job qualifications were. She moved to the front of the desk and took one of a pair of leather club chairs. Montana took the other. Sydney tried to appear nonchalant, but it was tough. Working for the illustrious Brubaker family would be a dream come true.

"Okay, Cindy. Why are you here, honey?" Big Daddy's puzzled frown took her aback.

"Big Daddy, I think Cindy is applying for the ranch hand job. Is that right, Cindy?" Montana's warm smile gave her confidence.

"Yes." She sat up a little straighter.

"Oh." Big Daddy scratched his jaw. "It was the clothes that threw me, I guess."

Sydney felt the tips of her ears grow hot. "I'd be dressed this way if I were interviewing for a janitorial position or a secretarial position. I believe in putting my best foot forward in any job interview."

"And you have."

There was approval in Montana's voice, and she found herself relaxing. "Anyway, I saw your ad in the paper, and I feel that I have the experience and qualifications for the job." She held out her folder to Big Daddy. "If you'll just take a moment, I think you'll see—"

"Right. Sure." The older man took the folder and, setting it on the ink blotter before him, crossed his hands over the top. "Paper is so impersonal. Go ahead, honey. Why do you want a foreman's assistant ranch hand job?"

Because it's all that's available, she wanted to scream. *Because I'm on the verge of losing my spread and I'm desperate for the money. Because all the really good ranch management jobs are currently taken by a bunch of less qualified men.*

But, she couldn't do that. Instead, she donned a confident smile and told a partial truth, "Because I see this position as an opportunity to hone my skills. Someday, I hope to run my own ranch." *Again.* She smiled so hard that the cords in her neck began to throb and her back teeth to ache.

"Ahh."

The ensuing silence was deafening. Sydney racked her brain for something else that would convince them that she was the only candidate for the job. Because this job was her best—and last—hope!

If you enjoyed what you just read,
then we've got an offer you can't resist!

Take 2 bestselling love stories FREE!

Plus get a FREE surprise gift!

Clip this page and mail it to Silhouette Reader Service™

IN U.S.A.	IN CANADA
3010 Walden Ave.	P.O. Box 609
P.O. Box 1867	Fort Erie, Ontario
Buffalo, N.Y. 14240-1867	L2A 5X3

YES! Please send me 2 free Silhouette Romance® novels and my free surprise gift. Then send me 6 brand-new novels every month, which I will receive months before they're available in stores. In the U.S.A., bill me at the bargain price of $2.90 plus 25¢ delivery per book and applicable sales tax, if any*. In Canada, bill me at the bargain price of $3.25 plus 25¢ delivery per book and applicable taxes**. That's the complete price and a savings of at least 10% off the cover prices—what a great deal! I understand that accepting the 2 free books and gift places me under no obligation ever to buy any books. I can always return a shipment and cancel at any time. Even if I never buy another book from Silhouette, the 2 free books and gift are mine to keep forever. So why not take us up on our invitation. You'll be glad you did!

215 SEN C24Q
315 SEN C24R

Name _____ (PLEASE PRINT) _____

Address _____ Apt.# _____

City _____ State/Prov. _____ Zip/Postal Code _____

* Terms and prices subject to change without notice. Sales tax applicable in N.Y.
** Canadian residents will be charged applicable provincial taxes and GST.
   All orders subject to approval. Offer limited to one per household.
   ® are registered trademarks of Harlequin Enterprises Limited.

SROM00_R   ©1998 Harlequin Enterprises Limited

Silhouette® —

where love comes alive—online...

eHARLEQUIN.com

your romantic life

—Romance 101—
♥ Guides to romance, dating and flirting.

—Dr. Romance—
♥ Get romance advice and tips from
our expert, Dr. Romance.

—Recipes for Romance—
♥ How to plan romantic meals for you
and your sweetie.

—Daily Love Dose—
♥ Tips on how to keep the romance
alive every day.

—Tales from the Heart—
♥ Discuss romantic dilemmas with other
members in our Tales from the Heart
message board.

You're not going to believe this offer!

In October and November 2000, buy any two Harlequin or Silhouette books and save $10.00 off future purchases, or buy any three and save $20.00 off future purchases!

Just fill out this form and attach 2 proofs of purchase (cash register receipts) from October and November 2000 books and Harlequin will send you a coupon booklet worth a total savings of $10.00 off future purchases of Harlequin and Silhouette books in 2001. Send us 3 proofs of purchase and we will send you a coupon booklet worth a total savings of $20.00 off future purchases.

Saving money has never been this easy.

I accept your offer! Please send me a coupon booklet:

Name: _____

Address: _____ City: _____

State/Prov.: _____ Zip/Postal Code: _____

Optional Survey!

In a typical month, how many Harlequin or Silhouette books would you buy <u>new</u> at retail stores?

☐ Less than 1　　☐ 1　　☐ 2　　☐ 3 to 4　　☐ 5+

Which of the following statements best describes how you <u>buy</u> Harlequin or Silhouette books? Choose one answer only that <u>best</u> describes you.

☐ I am a regular buyer and reader
☐ I am a regular reader but buy only occasionally
☐ I only buy and read for specific times of the year, e.g. vacations
☐ I subscribe through Reader Service but also buy at retail stores
☐ I mainly borrow and buy only occasionally
☐ I am an occasional buyer and reader

Which of the following statements best describes how you <u>choose</u> the Harlequin and Silhouette series books you buy <u>new</u> at retail stores? By "series," we mean books within a particular line, such as *Harlequin PRESENTS* or *Silhouette SPECIAL EDITION*. Choose one answer only that <u>best</u> describes you.

☐ I only buy books from my favorite series
☐ I generally buy books from my favorite series but also buy
　　books from other series on occasion
☐ I buy some books from my favorite series but also buy from
　　many other series regularly
☐ I buy all types of books depending on my mood and what
　　I find interesting and have no favorite series

Please send this form, along with your cash register receipts as proofs of purchase, to:
In the U.S.: Harlequin Books, P.O. Box 9057, Buffalo, NY 14269
In Canada: Harlequin Books, P.O. Box 622, Fort Erie, Ontario L2A 5X3

(Allow 4-6 weeks for delivery) Offer expires December 31, 2000.　　　　PHQ4002